Gossamer Summer

Gossamer Summer

H. M. Bouwman

A Atheneum Books for Young Readers
atheneum NEW YORK LONDON TORONTO SYDNEY NEW DELHI

ATHENEUM BOOKS FOR YOUNG READERS

An imprint of Simon & Schuster Children's Publishing Division

1230 Avenue of the Americas, New York, New York 10020

Text © 2023 by H. M. Bouwman

Jacket illustration © 2023 by Ji-Hyuk Kim

Jacket design by Greg Stadnyk © 2023 by Simon & Schuster, Inc.

ATHENEUM BOOKS FOR YOUNG READERS is a registered trademark of Simon & Schuster, Inc. Atheneum logo is a trademark of Simon & Schuster, Inc.

For information about special discounts for bulk purchases, please contact Simon & Schuster Special Sales at 1-866-506-1949 or business@simonandschuster.com.

The Simon & Schuster Speakers Bureau can bring authors to your live event. For more information or to book an event, contact the Simon & Schuster Speakers Bureau at 1-866-248-3049 or visit our website at www.simonspeakers.com.

Interior design by Irene Metaxatos

Manufactured in the United States of America

The text for this book was set in Cotford Text.

0423 FFG

First Edition

10 9 8 7 6 5 4 3 2 1

Library of Congress Cataloging-in-Publication Data

Names: Bouwman, H. M., author.

Title: Gossamer summer / H.M. Bouwman.

Description: First edition. | New York : Atheneum Books for Young Readers, [2023] | Audience: Ages 8 to 12. | Summary: Four sisters make a friend, find a grubby fairy, and defend the neighborhood against evil birds in this book about grief, magic, and the power of stories.

Identifiers: LCCN 2022027917 | ISBN 9781665912532 (hardcover) | ISBN 9781665912556 (ebook)

Subjects: CYAC: Sisters—Fiction. | Magic—Fiction. | Fairies—Fiction. | Grief—Fiction. | Storytelling—Fiction.

Classification: LCC PZ7.B6713 Go 2023 | DDC [Fic]—dc23

LC record available at https://lccn.loc.gov/2022027917

❦ ❦ ❦

As with all stories, this one is for G. and R.:
you builders of fairy gardens and curators of
creepy fossil collections and tellers of
strange tales. But even more, this book is for my
three beloved sisters, who are not very much
like Maisie, Bee, and Amy, except for the constant
and beautiful feeling of us standing
together against the world—and the thing
about the camidge.

Gossamer Summer

Something on the Lawn

It all started when Jojo saw a fairy but said she didn't.

Jojo sat on the rickety rocking chair on the long, wide porch, the first sister outside for the day. She was petting Fabio the cat and gazing dreamily at the small yellow house across the street. Other than their own big, white, almost-falling-down home, it was the only building on the dead-end road. An old man lived there—which meant that Jojo and her sisters ruled the neighborhood. Being in charge was maybe the only good thing about living out here in the middle of nowhere, far away from any other kids.

And, of course, far away from Grandma Nan.

But Jojo wasn't thinking about Grandma Nan right now. Nope. She squinted at the yellow house until it got all fuzzy. How should they spend their second day of summer vacation? Fabio rotated on her lap and nudged her for more petting.

And then she saw it. At first she didn't realize what it was. Something small flickered in the corner of her vision, something that winkled on the little stump where the twins had left a plate of food the night before, for the fairies. Jojo first thought, *Fabio is eating the fairy food, the naughty cat!*—but then she remembered the cat was curled on her lap.

It must be a squirrel, then. She leaned forward in her seat and stared. The creature was the size of a squirrel, but . . . was it green? And it looked like . . . well, from the back it looked almost like a very small person. Squirrel-sized. And—wearing a shirt?

It looked like a small person stuffing food into their muddy shirt.

Jojo squinted again, the sun in her eyes. It was a trick of the light. Had to be.

Fabio mewed and prickled his claws into Jojo's leg, making her jump. The creature turned around, saw her, and froze. It looked *exactly* like a small greenish person. And—with a beard made of *grass*?

The creature looked like a fairy from a story she'd once told her sisters, one in which the boy fairies all wore suspenders and had mossy greenish beards that grew halfway down their stomachs. *A grungy fairy?* But that was only pretend. And she didn't tell those stories anymore.

The small stranger nodded at Jojo. Like they knew each other. Then it waved its hand like it wanted her to come over and chat.

Just then a cupboard inside the house thumped, and at the same time a couple of birds flew overhead, cheeping, and the little creature ducked and raced off, tumbling across the street and around the yellow house to disappear into the woods behind it. Gone before Jojo could even breathe or yell or anything.

Fabio glared up at Jojo, tail twitching. He hopped off her lap, stalked over to a small pile of blankets, and recurled himself into a crescent roll.

Carefully Jojo stepped down from the porch and tiptoed over to the stump where her younger sisters had left their fairy presents. The grass was still morning-damp, and there was a faint trail of disturbed dew leading toward the road, exactly as if a squirrel-sized person had scampered off.

The stump was empty. The food and note the twins had put there were gone.

At that moment the twins slammed out the back door and ran noisily around the house to the front. Maisie, the oldest sister, banged outside after them, calling, "The cooler has *all* our food in it, and the water jug is heavy and it's for *all of us*, but I've got it. No one needs to help."

Jojo ignored her, and so did the twins.

Bee, the one-smidge-taller and seven-minutes-older twin, gasped and said, "It's gone! The delicious feast we made!"

"And the beautiful card we drew!" said Amy.

The delicious feast had been five-day-old fried rice the twins were supposed to take to the compost bin but instead arranged artfully on a paper plate, with fuzzy, shrunken strawberries on top. The beautiful card had been a handwritten note asking the fairies to visit the sisters in their new house, the paper scrap covered with splashes of red that looked like bloodstains.

"Did you see them?" Amy asked Jojo. "Were the fairies here when you came out?"

Jojo thought. She must have seen a squirrel. Yes, that was it. A mutant squirrel.

Amy gasped. "You *did*? You *saw them*? What did they look like?"

"What did they *smell* like?" Bee asked.

"No!" Jojo stepped back. "I didn't see anything."

The twins stared at her.

"But we asked, and you nodded—" started Amy.

"Fairies aren't real." Jojo needed time, alone with her brain, to think about what she'd imagined. "Anyway, it was Fabio."

"Fabio stole the fairy food?" Bee sounded wistful. "Did he . . . like it?"

"He ate the plate, too?" Amy sounded suspicious.

"He dragged it off. That direction, I think." Jojo gestured vaguely toward the backyard, away from the woods where the not-a-fairy had disappeared. "And the squirrels ate most of the food. One ran off when I came outside just now. Kind of a mutant one."

Jojo's younger sisters' shoulders slumped in unison. They weren't identical twins, but they looked the same, except that Bee was a tiny bit taller and had curlier hair, and Amy had more of a button nose and wider-set eyes, and Bee was right-handed and Amy left-handed, and Bee was more interested in food and slimy things, and Amy was more interested in art and crawly things. But otherwise: the same. They were five years old, the "little girls," while Maisie at eleven years old and Jojo at ten were the "big girls."

At least, that was what Grandma Nan had always called them. The little girls and the big girls. In the before time. Before last summer, when Grandma Nan died, and before last fall, when they moved out to the rambly house in the country.

"You're no fun anymore," said Amy. She ran to the porch, where their oldest sister had lugged the cooler and the water jug. "Maisie," she announced, "our fairy presents are gone!"

Maisie pushed the cooler against the front door. "And I bet they made the fairies happy. Now, do we have everything we need? Mom said not to come in at all today except to pee."

The four sisters looked around the porch, which ran across the whole front of the house. There were blankets and pillows to lie on, a stack of books and games and puzzles, a box of paper and crayons and pencils, a small wooden catapult, and a bucket of chalk. There was a bottle of soap for handwashing and some bandages for if you got scraped up. There was a skateboard and some old roller skates. There was one real chair—the rocking chair—which they had to take turns using. The cooler made a nice second chair if you sat on the lid and didn't bounce around too much. And of course, you could sprawl on the pillows and blankets.

The porch itself was lovely. The floor was graying wood that never gave splinters because the boards were fitted closely and worn smooth—good for pretend ice-skating if you remembered socks. Wide wooden steps led down to the lawn. Around three sides of the porch ran a metal railing you could stand on if you were brave, and you could hold on to the pillar at the porch's corner, lean forward, and pretend you were lookout on a pirate ship.

The porch had a big wooden door that was supposed to let you into the living room of the house. But the door didn't open, not ever, because it was one of those really old doors that needed a key in the inside lock, and the key had been lost long before they moved in, so they had to use the back door. The thing the porch door was good for was making a nice backrest for whoever sat on the cooler.

"Do we have everything?" Maisie asked again, looking at Jojo. Maisie didn't like it when she had to repeat things because someone was daydreaming.

"Socks?" said Jojo.

"Rats," Maisie said. "But that's not important enough to go back inside for." She took a small notebook and a pen out of the box of paper and wrote *socks for ice-skating* on the first blank page. "I'm making a list for tomorrow."

"Put candy on the list too. Tomorrow should have candy," said Bee.

Maisie ignored her and put the list back in the

paper box. "Plans for today?" She looked at Jojo. "General?"

"Thank you, President," said Jojo. "Today our plans are to land on Mars and—"

"We did that yesterday," said Amy.

"Yesterday was the moon. Day two is Mars."

"Same thing." Amy pouted out her bottom lip. "I want to do something different."

"Fine," Jojo said, crossing her arms on her chest like she imagined a real general might, just before he said, *Chop off their heads.* "Tell me what you want, underlings."

"First, don't call us underlings," said Amy. "Second, you're a nincompoopy—"

"No swearing," said Maisie.

And then Amy said the thing that Jojo thought she might say, the thing Jojo absolutely didn't want. "Let's play fairies!"

Bee said, "Yes! Because of the fairy presents getting eaten."

Jojo shook her head. No. They hadn't played fairies since Grandma Nan.

"That sounds like a great idea," said Maisie, glancing at Jojo with a question in her eyes. "With a fairy story, of course."

No no no.

The View from the Pirate Ship

More than all the other possible things Jojo didn't want to do, she especially didn't want to play fairies. Not today, not ever.

The sisters used to play fairies all the time with Grandma Nan, starting when Maisie and Jojo were toddlers and lasting until the past summer. Grandma Nan had lived in the apartment right next to them in town. She had taken care of them whenever Mom was working. And she'd loved Jojo's stories. Almost every day she'd ask what the fairies were doing, and Jojo would make up new adventures.

Last summer, the morning of the day when

everything started going wrong, they had taken a walk with Grandma Nan and found a dead baby bird on the sidewalk. It had fallen out of a tree, Grandma explained. They stooped to study the small, motionless mound. The baby eyelids looked bluish and naked, and the head was ruffled and wet-looking. The bird's body was pink and covered in fuzz because it was too new to have feathers. Jojo imagined the delicate skull and wing bones beneath the skin. Birds were such fragile things; when you saw one up close like this, it was hard to imagine how they ever lived.

"There's the nest," said Maisie, pointing at a spindly city maple.

Jojo looked up. What must the mother bird think?

Bee and Amy wanted to pick up the corpse and take it home. "So we can have a funeral," explained Amy.

But Grandma Nan said no, not this time. It wasn't hot out, but she was sweating and breathing kind of hard. "The city will come and pick it up."

"And have a funeral?" said Bee.

Grandma nodded, which was strange, because cities didn't have bird funerals, and Grandma didn't usually lie. "Let's go back now. I'm afraid I need a nap."

Maisie took Grandma's arm, suddenly worried. "Are you okay?" Jojo took her other arm. Grandma Nan's skin felt hot.

At the apartment, Grandma went to her bedroom to lie down, and the sisters sat on her living room floor, not sure what to do. Grandma never needed naps.

"We should do something quiet," said Maisie. "So she can rest."

Amy and Bee got out paper and crayons. They wanted to draw the dead bird. "Joey," said Bee, "tell us a story while we draw. That way we'll remember to be quiet."

So Jojo did. Even now, so much later, she remembered that story—because it was the last fairy story she told. There was an army of dead birds, but they didn't have ruffled fuzz or blue eyelids; they were skeletons, flying around and searching for a fairy village to attack. Bee and Amy shivered, repeating Jojo's sentences after she said them, like they were a poem the little girls wanted to memorize. The bone birds were terrifying, and the fairies were brave but overwhelmed. What would happen?

But Jojo never finished telling. Maisie slipped back to the bedroom to check on Grandma, and when she returned, she interrupted the story. "We need to get Mom." Mom was working in their apartment next door. They weren't supposed to bother her unless it was an emergency. "It's an emergency," said Maisie.

And that was it. Grandma Nan was really sick. She went away, and they never saw her again, because she died. The whole time Grandma Nan was in the hospital—for almost two weeks—Jojo talked to the fairies, quietly, in her head. She asked the fairies to use their magic to make Grandma Nan better.

But the fairies never did.

Because they weren't real. They were just a silly story.

Now, though, Bee was talking about how she wanted to play fairies, and Amy was saying she wanted to play too. Maisie joined in. "Maybe you can tell us . . . a story about them?" she suggested to Jojo. "Like you used to?"

Jojo tried to ignore everyone. They could play pirates today.

"Jojo?" Maisie said, in her nicest and most reasonable voice, the one that was hard to ignore.

Jojo tied a bandana around her head. "I don't feel like reading right now. Maisie can do it."

"Not from a book," said Amy. "A made-up story."

"Like the olden days," said Bee, "when we lived in the apartment in town."

"I don't remember any of those stories. Let's play pirates." Jojo scrambled up to stand on the railing of the porch. She was the only sister who could balance on the wobbly metal rail without immediately falling.

Amy growled.

Maisie said, "I have an idea. We can build fairy gardens. We don't need stories for that."

"Ahoy!" said Jojo. "A ship approaches! Hoist the skull and crossbones!"

"Jojo can have the spot under the pine tree for her fairy garden," said Maisie. That was the best place to build a fairy garden, as it was protected from the rain. "And Bee and Amy can have any other spots—"

"That's not fair," said Amy. "Under the tree is the best."

"And Amy and I are going to build ours together," said Bee, "so we should get the good spot."

Maisie said, "Well . . ."

"I don't want the stinky pine tree," said Jojo. "I'm playing pirates."

Maisie sighed. Loudly. "What if we do fairy gardens now and pirates after lunch?"

Jojo shrugged and kept watching for ships. Her sisters could build dorky fairy gardens if they wanted, but she wasn't going to.

"Great!" said Maisie. "Then let's get started."

"But we need a story first," said Bee. "It's part of the game."

Bee was not wrong. When they all used to make

fairy gardens with Grandma Nan, Jojo had always told a fairy story before they started, and the story always gave them ideas for their gardens, and when they finished, part of the fun was to see how each person's garden turned out the same or different from the story.

"Well," said Maisie after a short, heavy silence, "I think . . . we can use an old story."

The twins thought. "Were there any with candy?" asked Bee. "We *could* sneak back inside the house very, very quietly and get—"

"No," said Maisie. "How about the story with the fairies who have gossamer wings?"

"I don't remember that one," said Amy.

Jojo remembered. But she wasn't participating. She straightened her back and stared across the lawn. Maybe this ocean had sea monsters. Or an island with buried treasure.

"The gossamer-wing fairies sang lovely songs, and they danced, and they wore flower crowns in the moonlight. And they had gossamer wings," said Maisie. "Isn't that a good story?"

"What's gossamer?" said Bee.

"That's not a story," said Amy. "It's just a bunch of fats." She meant *facts*.

"Gossamer," said Maisie, "is . . . I'm not sure, exactly. Jojo, what's gossamer?"

Jojo wrapped both arms around the ship's mast and leaned her head against it, watching the stormy sea and wishing there really were enemies sailing toward them, something terrifying that would make them all run to aim the cannons. *Gossamer* was a Grandma Nan word. Jojo kind of knew what it meant. But she couldn't explain it, not like a dictionary would. Gossamer wings were . . . what were they? Wafty and delicate. Like gossip but without the meanness.

"Anyway," said Maisie, who seemed to be finally giving up on Jojo, "gossamer is beautiful. Let's do that story."

"It's not a story," said Amy again. "It's just a list of stuff about fairies."

"Ohhh!" said Bee. "Let's do the one with the bone creatures. Remember?"

Of course they all remembered it: Jojo's last fairy story. Even now, almost a year after Grandma Nan had died, Bee and Amy sometimes still repeated their favorite lines to each other, like memorized bits of a scary campfire tale. On top of all that, yesterday— the first official day of summer—they had found a bird skeleton in their backyard: a delicate head and beak. They'd buried it under a mound of leaves. So of course they all remembered a year ago.

"'Numberless bone creatures flapped across the sky,'" said Bee.

"'Their skeletal wings creaking,'" added Amy. They remembered the words exactly.

"Jojo?" said Maisie. And when Jojo didn't answer, Maisie said, "Okay, then. Let's each build any fairy garden we want. From any story we want."

"Twins are building together," said Bee.

"And we already have an idea," said Amy.

"So do I," said Maisie. She cleared her throat. "What about you, Jojo?"

There *was* a ship sailing toward them: a car, coming down the dead-end road toward their house. Not a trick of light or a mutant squirrel or a figment of Jojo's imagination. A plain black car—not the neighbor's, which was red—was driving toward their house.

Jojo leaned forward to see better, lost her hold on the porch pillar, and tumbled into the mulch and weeds.

"Jojo?"

"Someone's coming," she said, jumping up and brushing off her shorts. "For real."

The girls all looked. The car slowed, pulled into the driveway of the little yellow house across the street, and drove behind the house, disappearing from view.

Jojo said, "There was someone in the back seat. A kid."

"Are you sure?" said Maisie. "I didn't see anyone."

There hadn't been a kid at the yellow house before, not for the whole fall and winter and spring they'd lived on this street. It had been only them. "I'm *sure* I saw someone," Jojo said. "Someone short."

Maisie sat on the porch step and tilted her head in thought. "Maybe the old man has a grandkid?"

They waited, hoping to see the kid, if there was one. But no one appeared. The people in the car must have gone in the back door of the yellow house. The kid, if there was one, did not come outside.

Bee and Amy flopped back on the floor of the porch, their heads together to make a V with their bodies. "When is lunchtime?" said Bee.

Maisie patted the porch step for Jojo to sit next to her. "Are you sure it wasn't just a really short grown-up?"

"In the back seat?"

"Good point," said Maisie.

If it *was* a kid, they needed to—

"If there's someone there," said Maisie, "then we need to do something interesting that'll make them see us and want to come over."

Jojo stared at her. Exactly what she'd been thinking.

At that moment the black car backed out of the yellow house's driveway and drove away. The driver looked like a man, but not the old man who lived in the house. The back seat was now empty.

They all sat in silence for a minute, thinking.

"Let's act out a fairy story," said Bee. "Like a play. That will make the kid want to come out."

Ugh. There was no way Jojo was acting in a play about fairies. But if her sisters made fairy gardens, at least she could build something else. Whatever she wanted. "Fairy *gardens*," she said.

"And after gardens, let's play tag," said Maisie.

Jojo nodded. That would bring the kid outside. Who could resist building things and running?

A Stranger Arrives

Have you ever built a fairy garden? It's made with small things you find outside, and the key is to make it beautiful and cozy so that fairies want to stop by while you're sleeping. When you wake up in the morning, you'll know they visited, because they leave gifts behind: pretty rocks, or a little blue feather, or a perfect spiral shell. Things like that. My sisters and I used to build fairy gardens when we went camping, and once the fairies even brought—

But this story is about Maisie and Jojo and Bee and Amy—so I'll get back to them.

The four girls spent the rest of their morning

building fairy gardens. Or, to be more accurate: Maisie and Bee and Amy built fairy gardens, and Jojo built something else.

Jojo built a fort for her action figures, which included a faded green Hulk, a He-Man who'd lost a leg, a woman made out of pieces of a magnet set (she tended to fall apart when bumped, but she was the only woman superhero Jojo had), and a creepy headless swamp creature who always had to be the villain because: no head. The fort had walls made of sticks and a moat and a high platform to shoot arrows from.

Maisie built a bark mansion that you could almost imagine creatures with gossamer wings living in, all fragile and wispy. It had moss carpets, flower-jeweled sofas, and chairs made of shells she'd collected at a lake a long time ago and usually kept in a jar in the bedroom but that she'd brought to the porch yesterday.

Beach shells were kind of cheating, but Jojo didn't feel like arguing about it. Anyway, her superhero fort was almost done. She cartwheeled across the lawn. "We need to be more interesting to watch," she said to Maisie. "Like the littles."

Amy and Bee kept darting from under the pine tree, running behind the house, and returning, still running, carrying mysterious things in their hands.

"Fine," said Maisie. She cartwheeled away to pick more violets for her sofas.

While they were building the gardens (and superhero fort), Fabio the cat hunted a robin. He hunted birds a lot but never caught any, because even though he looked sleek and enormously muscly, he was too slow. That was why Fabio was allowed outside—because he couldn't live up to his murderous tendencies.

Finally he gave up and curled into a ball on the porch and fell asleep.

Maisie returned with a handful of drooping violets. "I'm making a castle that a human queen would like. I mean if she was really tiny," she said to Jojo. "Remember the story about the fairies and the human queen?"

"Like Narnia," Jojo said, adding sticks to her fort. Long ago Mom had read them the Narnia book. She used to read aloud every night (except when she was on deadline). Amy and Bee were too little then to really listen, but Jojo and Maisie loved the Narnia book—even the White Witch, who was powerful enough to make snow. But what Jojo and Maisie loved best was the idea that four siblings could become rulers of a magical country.

Maisie repeated softly, "Remember the human queen?"

Jojo remembered.

Amy swerved around them, returning from the backyard again. "Oh! Human queen!" She scooted under the pine tree and huddled with Bee.

"And remember how you made up a story about the human queen and the fairies?" said Maisie. "I liked that one so much. There was a throne and everything."

"I don't remember that," said Jojo. But she remembered. She'd started telling it one day when Grandma Nan was taking care of them, and Grandma had said it was a lovely story and she wanted to hear the rest of it. But Jojo had never gotten around to finishing that story because they'd started playing something else—and now Grandma Nan would never get to hear the rest.

"How did that story end?" asked Maisie, kneeling to make a new flower sofa.

Jojo shrugged. "It didn't. It was pointless."

Maisie looked up at Jojo, hurt, and for a moment Jojo felt a twinge of sorry.

Then Bee yelled, "And the *bone creatures*!" and Amy ran again to the backyard. Fabio slowly rose from his nap, stretched, and loped over to Bee under the pine tree.

Maisie stood up, suspicious. "What exactly are you two doing?"

"You'll see when it's all done," Bee said. "Don't come yet."

Amy returned, walking sideways and hiding something behind her back so her older sisters couldn't see. She stooped under the tree, giggling. Then Bee shooed Fabio away from their masterpiece, which he was trying to eat.

When Maisie said time was up, Bee said she was starving.

Jojo picked up Fabio, and they all headed toward the front porch, where their food sat in its Styrofoam cooler. Fabio, disgruntled, jumped down and wandered back into the grass to stalk a spider.

But as the girls started up the porch steps, there was a voice behind them. "What're you all doing?"

Standing on their lawn, having appeared from what seemed like nowhere, was a stranger. The stranger was almost exactly the same height as Jojo and had short, dark hair and was wearing brand-new sneakers with no dirt and no holes.

"Are you a boy?" asked Maisie, because of course you never knew without asking.

The boy nodded.

Jojo said, "Are you the kid from across the street? Is he your grandpa?"

Amy said, "We made fairy gardens, and we're going to have lunch now."

Bee elbowed her. "Don't talk to strangers," she whispered very loudly.

The strange boy looked at her.

"He asked what we're doing," said Amy, "and I'm the only one who answered. I think that makes me the polite sister."

The boy cleared his throat.

"WAIT," said Jojo. "Let him talk."

They all closed their mouths and stared at their visitor. Maisie seated herself in the rocker. Amy and Bee plopped down on the porch steps, and Amy tapped her foot like she was tired of waiting. Jojo stayed standing on the grass next to the steps.

The boy took a deep breath. "I'm here because— but he's not my grandpa."

"You're here because he's not your grandpa?" said Jojo. That didn't make any sense.

"No," said the boy. "I'm here for the summer. With my uncle, not my grandpa."

"Oh," said Maisie, rocking. "That makes more sense."

Bee said, "Your uncle is super old. Do you want some lunch?"

"What's your name?" asked Amy.

"Theo. And yes for lunch."

They had only one sandwich and one apple per girl, but when Maisie said, slowly, that she *could* go back into the house to get more food, Theo said, "I'll get something from my uncle." He ran across the empty street and into the little yellow house, then returned a minute later with a banana in one hand and a bagel in the other.

"But what's a fairy garden?" he asked, huffing and puffing. "What were you doing in the yard all morning, digging and cartwheeling and stuff?"

Jojo and Maisie looked at each other. Their plan had worked! He was here!

"We'll show you," Maisie said. "Put your food in the cooler or Fabio will eat it."

Bee sighed. "I guess we can have lunch after."

While Theo stowed his food, they told him all their names and ages—and found out he was ten, like Jojo—and then they walked around the yard to show the fairy gardens (and the superhero fort).

Jojo's fort, made of sticks and pebbles, had an empty moat all around the outside, to protect the superheroes from attackers. When it was filled with water, the moat would have alligators in it.

"The alligators keep the superheroes safe," said Theo, understanding immediately.

Jojo nodded.

"Who wants to attack the superheroes?"

Jojo shrugged. "Cats. Caterpillars. You never know."

"An alligator moat won't keep out bone creatures," Bee murmured.

"Bone creatures?" said Theo.

"They can fly," said Amy.

Next they looked at Maisie's mansion. It was mostly moss and leaves and flowers, and of course the pearly shells. Jojo thought it needed a moat, but Maisie said, "My fairies never fight, though. They just . . . sing . . . and weave things and fall in love. They have gossamer wings," she added.

Bee and Amy shrugged, but Theo nodded like he was pretending he knew what that meant.

Lastly, they all ducked under the pine tree to see the twins' garden. It was shaded and cool under the tree, and the air was still, like being inside a tent. Near the trunk, they could all stand without hitting their heads on the downward-slanting branches, even Maisie.

The twins' fairy garden was . . .

"Uh, what is that?" asked Maisie, pointing.

"And that?" said Jojo, also pointing.

"And that green stuff?" said Theo. He didn't even have to point.

"The green stuff is fairy throw-up," said Amy. "We tore leaves into tiny pieces and added muddy water. One of the fairies threw up after killing a bone creature."

"The throw-up is my favorite part of the garden," said Bee. "Is it yours, too?"

Theo didn't answer, or if he did, they didn't notice, because Amy was talking again. "Here's the empty throne waiting for the new human queen to arrive from our world. The red stuff is crushed berries, which is blood from the fairy queen who just died a cruel, cruel death."

"We mashed berries all over to make blood everywhere," said Bee cheerfully.

"You have a queen who just died a cruel death?" asked Maisie in a strangled voice.

Bee nodded. "A cruel, *cruel* death. She was killed by the bone creatures. Over here." She gently stroked the centerpiece of their garden. It was the tiny bird skull they had found yesterday. "Bone creatures are numberless. This is the only one the fairies defeated."

Jojo blinked. "But that's not how . . ." The bird from the backyard wasn't a bone creature. And anyway, that wasn't how the story had gone. It didn't have a queen in it.

"We remember the lines," said Amy. "'Numberless bone creatures flapped across the sky, their skeletal wings creaking, as they scouted for a fairy village to attack and pillage, which they did each week—'"

"Stop it," said Jojo. "It's not a story."

"Only because you didn't finish it," said Maisie reasonably.

"We added some stuff," said Amy, "to make a story. We added the queen. And the blood."

"And the throw-up," said Bee.

"And a dead bone creature. See, the fairies lost this battle. There's a lot of blood." Amy dabbed a little more mulberry juice on the bird skull. Her fingers were purple.

"Well," said Maisie before Jojo could say anything, "your garden is imaginative, that's for sure."

Bee said, "I'm *starving*."

Maisie made them all wash their hands with lots of soap under the spigot—especially any hands that had played with skulls, she said—and then they sat on the porch to eat. Maisie opened the cooler and handed out food, which was always her job, since she was the fairest food-hander-outer. The cooler was an old Styrofoam hospital container with a sticker on the side that said HUMAN ORGANS, and it held the apples and sandwiches—and now Theo's bagel and banana too. There was one big bottle of water that the sisters shared. Theo put his face under the spigot to drink.

Maisie had made their sandwiches early that morning. The sisters were supposed to stay outside all day except for quietly using the bathroom. Because of Mom's deadline.

When they all had eaten—and had emptied the water bottle and refilled it from the spigot and then drunk most of it again—Jojo read aloud the next chapter of their book, which they kept on the porch along with the blankets and pillows, for whenever they had to spend the day outside. Amy and Bee lay down to listen, and Bee fell asleep before the chapter was over, so Jojo had to wake her and reread the last page.

Theo had never heard the story before, but he could tell what it was about. Some kids had found a strange creature buried in the ground, and it gave them wishes. He wondered aloud if that could ever happen in real life.

"Not likely," said Amy. "More likely a fairy or what-ever would *take* wishes from you. Don't you think?"

"I don't know what you mean," said Maisie. "Fair-ies are nothing but kind."

"Unless they curse you," said Bee, still sleepy.

"Well," said Theo, "I'd rather be visited by the wish-granting kind." His face wrinkled like he knew a wish he'd make.

Jojo put the book back in the basket on the porch. If you just assumed, she thought, that fairies were characters in books—not real people, *which they weren't*—her sisters had good points. In books, fair-ies seemed to . . . change from book to book, almost like people couldn't agree what they were really like. It was confusing. When Jojo used to tell stories, she kept her fairies kind of the same: brave and strong, fighting off scary creatures, and never throwing up in battle.

Until now. Until Amy and Bee took her old story and tinkered with it.

Anyway, fairies weren't real, not even if it *looked* like one was eating your leftover fried rice and moldy strawberries. And now that Jojo had built a fort and met a new kid and eaten lunch and read a book, what she'd seen that morning seemed even less real. Just pretend.

The rest of the day passed quickly. The five kids added more items to the fairy gardens and the superhero fort; they played hide-and-seek in Theo's uncle's backyard, which was far bigger than their own; and they showed off their cartwheels for one another.

Then Theo's uncle called him in to supper, and Maisie said, "We better go inside too." And they all sighed, because there were breakfast dishes waiting to be washed, and supper that would probably not taste good, and then showers and bed. Mom would be there too, but Mom on deadline was not nearly as fun as Mom not on deadline.

"Will you play outside tomorrow?" asked Theo.

"Of course," said Jojo. "Right away in the morning. We'll be outside all day."

"We can check on the fairy houses then," said Bee.

Theo said, "Check on them?"

"To see if the fairies visited," said Amy. "And left presents."

They wouldn't have. Grandma Nan had always been the one who left gifts from the fairies.

Theo's uncle called again.

"See you tomorrow!" said Theo. "I'll bring my lunch!"

Maisie and Bee and Amy cleaned up the porch, moving things away from the edge so that if it rained tonight, the blankets and books wouldn't get wet. Jojo stayed at the bottom of the steps and watched Theo run across the road and into the yellow house. Then, suddenly, her attention was caught by a quick movement.

In the far bushes near the woods, something small and greenish and personlike nodded at her, blinked its eyes, rustled the leaves, and disappeared.

4

The Pretend Librarian

Grandma Nan had always said that Jojo was a great storyteller. But Jojo's stories had mostly been about fairies, which she was done with, so she needed to find another job. This past year Maisie had become the responsible and good-mannered sister—and the worrier. The twins weren't really finished forming, like a pudding that hasn't firmed up yet, so it was hard to tell how they would turn out, but if they followed their current interests, they would probably work with mud and boogers. Crossing out "responsible," "good-mannered," "worry," "mud," and "boogers" still left Jojo with a lot of career choices.

Jojo wasn't a great speller or a great sandwich maker or a great dishwasher or a great go-to-bedder. (She always snuck a book to bed, and she read under the moonlight or with a flashlight, even though Mom—when she remembered—said not to.) But back when she used to tell stories, she'd been a great storyteller. It didn't even matter what kind of story. Sometimes one of her sisters would start—like, say, by building a fairy garden in which the fairy queen had been killed and there was blood and throw-up on the ground—and in the old days, Jojo would immediately create an entire story, and it would make sense and everything. I mean, it would make sense the way the best fairy stories do: not that it could really happen, but that it *felt* like it could really happen.

If she wasn't going to be a great storyteller any-more, Jojo needed to be great at something else. She had standards to live up to.

Sitting on the porch in the late-afternoon sun, Jojo sniffed, inhaled a gnat, and rubbed at her nose, blowing out fiercely to try to expel it before it ate all the way through her nose parts and into her skull and then colonized her brain, turning her into a zombie. Maisie said, "Use a Kleenex," and Amy said, "What kind of bug was it?" and Bee said, "Bug boogers!" and Jojo felt suddenly tired, like she'd gone invisible a long time ago but only just now realized that no one could see her.

From inside the house, a cupboard slammed shut. The shades in the front windows popped up. Footsteps moved on the creaky floors. The house had been sleeping all day and was now waking.

"That's supper," said Bee.

"Let's go help," said Maisie.

At supper the sisters told Mom about the new boy, and they all agreed that Theo was a good addition to their games. "He's really just as good as a girl, I think," said Amy, tossing her head.

"That's sexist," said Maisie.

"Is not," said Amy. "I said he was just as good."

Maisie shook her head.

"What else did you do today?" asked Mom.

They told Mom about playing tag and hide-and-seek. They didn't tell her much about the fairy gardens. Jojo didn't want to talk about fairies, and for some reason Maisie didn't seem to want to explain about the twins' garden; she glared at Amy when Amy started describing it, and then she turned the discussion to Theo again. So most of the talk was about Theo, who was much more interesting than a fairy garden anyway.

Jojo wasn't sure why Maisie thought Mom wouldn't like the twins' garden, but Maisie usually understood grown-ups better than Jojo did. Maisie was probably right.

Today Mom looked more tired than usual, resting her chin in one hand between bites. Her hair was a little bit gray right where it came out from her head, because she hadn't dyed it over the sink in a few weeks. The gray had just happened this past year, and Mom said she didn't like it yet but maybe she would like it in ten years, which didn't make sense to Jojo. Either you liked something or you didn't.

Mom didn't talk about how her day had gone, and she wasn't listening very hard either. She was eating the burnt hotdish and the mushy corn, and she was staring off into space, moving her mouth once in a while like she was thinking about something far away.

Finally Maisie said, "Is your writing going well?"

And Mom jerked her head a little, like she was waking up, and looked at the four girls. She took off her glasses and rubbed at her eyes. "Yes, I think so. I think so. Deadline in a couple of days. And just a few more chapters to rewrite."

"What is the woman's name in this book?" asked Amy.

"And what is the other person's?" asked Bee.

Mom smiled, putting her glasses back on. "Willow. And Vlad."

"And they're going to get married?"

"If I can convince them to fall in love." She sighed and disappeared back into her daydream.

"Willow and Vlad," said Jojo, trying to imagine. Willow was a tree. Was Vlad a tree too? Was Vlad even a real name? Or was it made up, like fairies?

The little green stranger darted into her mind.

When Jojo came back from her thoughts, she'd eaten most of her burnt hotdish and Mom was talking again. ". . . just a couple more days outside. You all are being so helpful. And I'm writing so much. I know it's not like when Grandma Nan took care of you—"

Jojo stood up. "I'm done. Can I be excused?"

Mom blinked, then nodded. "Clear the table, please." Slowly she went back into her daydream over her plate.

The next morning the four girls ate their cereal and milk quickly and quietly, rinsed the bowls and put them in the sink until after supper, and ran outside with their lunch packed in the cooler. Bee and Amy and Jojo were all wearing the same clothes from yesterday, because it took too much time to find clean things. Maisie wore a clean shirt but the same shorts, and she carried the cooler.

When they came around to the front of the house, Theo was already sitting on the porch, on top of a blanket, waiting for them. They put his food in the cooler too—a sandwich and an orange and a baggie full of carrot sticks. "My uncle said to share the carrots for a snack."

Amy said, "Do we have to?" but after Maisie glared at her, she added, "Thankyouverymuch."

"In that case," said Jojo, "we might as well eat our vegetables now and get it over with." She divided them up—three sticks per kid—and they all bravely crunched away.

"Carrots are good for you," said Maisie to encourage them all.

"Carrots are what bone creatures eat," muttered Amy.

Jojo and Maisie ate quickly, and Theo ate at a normal speed, but it took a long time for Amy and Bee to finish their carrots. While everyone else waited for the twins to finish, Jojo said, "Tell us your life, Theo. Why are you staying with your uncle this summer?"

Maisie nudged her and whispered, "That might not be polite to ask." But then she looked at Theo like she still wanted him to answer.

"It's okay," said Theo. "I don't mind." But he looked kind of like he *did* mind. Fabio came over and nuzzled his shoulder, and he petted the giant cat. Then he took a big breath. "I'm staying with my uncle because my dad works until almost bedtime every day, and my mom is—she's in Greenland this summer doing research. She's a scientist."

"She's in Greenland?" Jojo wasn't exactly sure where that was, but it sounded far away and amazing. "What's it like there?"

Theo nodded like he liked her question. "Greenland has a lot of ice and snow," he said. "Which is weird since they named it *Green*land. My mom told me that in the summer, the sun shines almost all night long. She's living in a tent on the ice, and she has to wear special boots for walking around."

"Where does she go pee?" asked Bee with her mouth full of carrot.

"Gross," said Maisie.

"In a special outhouse," said Theo. "But it's super cold."

Bee shuddered. She didn't like cold bathrooms.

"What about you?" asked Theo. "Where are . . . your parents?" He paused, like he thought maybe it was odd that they packed a medical cooler with food and spent all day outside.

But it wasn't odd. It was because Mom was on deadline, and she needed them to leave her alone and pretend like they were camping so she could write. Later, when her book was done, she would email it to her editor, clean the house, and say, "What would you girls like to do today?" and they'd go for a hike in the woods together or maybe bake pretzels in the shapes of animals, or something else fun. But deadline weeks, which happened several times every year, were hard to explain.

Deadline weeks used to be *especially* fun because Grandma Nan would take them to the museum or the park or the library and then bring them to her apartment and make them grilled cheese sandwiches and tomato soup and read them books and send them home at bedtime with a dish of food for their mom.

But now deadlines were harder. This past year had been Maisie and Jojo's first without Grandma Nan to meet them after school each day, and it was the twins' first year of prekindergarten; and for all of them it was their first year living in the big house outside of town and having to take a bus to school; *and* Mom had been trying to write her books and pay all the bills. A lot of things got forgotten this past year, like reading journals that were supposed to be signed and go back to the teacher, and the wearing of hats and mittens on cold days, and once Maisie even forgot to pack lunches for everyone. She cried that day because she felt so bad about it, even though Mom said it wasn't Maisie's fault, since parents were supposed to be in charge of lunches.

Jojo and her sisters were lucky that this writing deadline was happening in the summer, because during the school year there were a lot more things to mess up than just heating up a hotdish for supper.

Maisie poked Jojo and brought her back from her daydream. "Hey. Theo asked about our parents." She turned to Theo and answered him. "We don't have a dad."

"We have *two* dads," said Amy. "One dad for Maisie and Jojo, and a different dad for me and Bee. But we only see Bee's and my dad. Every other weekend, me and Bee go see him."

"That's why Maisie and Jojo are so pale," said Bee. "Different dad."

"Ghost dad," said Amy.

Theo nodded like he understood, but his face said he didn't.

"It's not really that complicated," said Amy.

They sat in silence for a moment. The littles wandered off with their remaining carrots.

"What about your mom?" said Theo. "Isn't she . . .

I mean, doesn't she take care of you?" He glanced toward Bee and Amy, whose hair stuck out in all directions and whose shorts were stained with mulberries from yesterday. They were now spitting carrot juice off the porch to see who could spit the farthest. Amy was winning.

Suddenly Jojo felt like their life wasn't good enough. Theo had a mom who was living with polar bears and exploring the arctic, basically, and what did they have but a mom who was writing a book with kissing in it that they weren't even allowed to read? "We don't—we don't have a mom," said Jojo.

"What?" said Maisie. Amy and Bee turned to stare, Amy with carrot juice running down her chin.

"We can trust Theo," said Jojo, glaring at the little girls with the special glare that said, *Don't ruin the story*. She glared at Maisie, too, just to be sure, and Maisie narrowed her eyes but didn't say anything.

"So, we're orphans," said Jojo. "Like the Boxcar Children. Did you ever read that book?"

Theo nodded. "It's a bunch of books."

"Well, we're like them, except we found an old, abandoned house instead of a boxcar, and we live in it, and every once in a while we sell a jewel that we found in a hoard in the basement, and then we can buy food."

"A story!" said Bee, clapping her hands. Jojo glared at her again, and she stopped immediately. "I mean, yes, that is all true and not a made-up story at all."

"And we buy water," said Maisie, helping out. "I mean, we sometimes sell a jewel so we can pay the water bill."

Jojo shook her head at Maisie, just a quick shiver of a headshake, to tell her to stop talking. Maisie was terrible at lying. Who cared about the water bill?

Theo shifted on his blanket, careful to keep his shoes off it. "But—my uncle said something about your mom. . . ."

"That's not our mom," said Jojo. "That's—that's a librarian. One of the librarians from town. She knows our secret and she sometimes stops by just to visit and check on us. Sometimes she brings us a hot dinner."

"We aren't old enough to use the oven unsupervised," said Maisie.

Really, Maisie was going to give everything away. "Of course we are," said Jojo. "Who would stop us? But we're too busy doing other things. So sometimes the librarian stops by, and when your uncle is in the yard, sometimes we even call her Mom, to keep our secret. Because no one can know that we live here all by ourselves."

"Why not?"

"They'd send us back to the orphanage. Which is run by a terrible woman who locks kids in closets when they misbehave. Closets with spikes."

"That sounds like a book I once read," said Theo. "With a girl who had magic brain powers."

"It is just like that book," said Jojo. "In fact, I think that book is based on the orphanage we escaped from." The story was getting away from her a little bit, and she felt like she needed to stop. "So, to conclude, we're hoping you can keep a secret, and not tell your uncle that the librarian isn't actually our mom."

Theo nodded.

"That was a good one, Joey," said Bee.

Maisie elbowed Bee.

Then Amy giggled, and Bee looked like she might start giggling too. Maisie said quickly, "So how about we look at the fairy gardens? We can see if the fairies visited."

"Presents!" yelled Bee. Amy clapped.

Grandma Nan was the one who used to leave gifts from the fairies. Maisie knew that. Who did she think was going to leave gifts?

Maisie gulped, like she just realized she'd said something foolish. "Oh, I mean, let's just look at the gardens again, before we do other things." To the twins she added, "The fairies were probably too busy to visit this time. The beginning of summer is . . . a really busy time of year for them. . . ."

But the twins had already run ahead to the lawn, whooping.

And, as it turned out, the fairy gardens *had* been visited.

5

A Letter for the Fairies

Gifts had been left in Jojo's fort and Maisie's mansion, not the kinds of gifts the girls usually got, but at least nice. Instead of the special rocks or little shells Grandma Nan had always left them, the floors of Maisie's mansion were now carpeted in a thick layer of petals that looked and smelled like roses. Where in the world had they come from? And all around Jojo's fort, the moat was now filled with muddy water—even though it had not rained last night. Sticking out of the water was a rock that was shaped almost exactly like an alligator. It was so real, it looked like it was glaring at you, about to open its jaws and bite.

The strangest (and most disturbing) garden, though, was the one belonging to the twins. On top of the mashed mulberries that the two girls had scattered yesterday, there lay a bunch of feathers, as if a cat had fought ferociously with a bird—and won. And on *top* of the feathers was something that looked like blood, but more purplish.

The scene under the pine tree was, in a word, ominous.

"Ominous," said Jojo. She knew this word. "An omen of something bad." She studied the carnage. The reddish purple on top of the feathers was mulberries—she could see the tiny seeds—though from far away it had definitely looked like blood.

"Maybe Fabio caught a bird?" said Theo.

"Fabio doesn't catch birds," said Jojo. "He's never even gotten close."

"He's too slow," said Maisie.

They stared in silence. Feathers, with mulberries crushed on top.

"Oh!" said Amy suddenly. "It's just like Jojo's story!"

Bee nodded, eyes wide. "The bone creatures . . ."

Maisie looked closer at the feather mess, shaking her head. "It's a coincidence. These are *bird* feathers. Birds aren't the same as bone creatures. Bone creatures are just . . . bone. Remember?" She gestured at the skull like it proved her point. Then she turned to Jojo and said, in a slightly accusing voice, "In your story the bone creatures didn't have feathers. So these *can't* be from a bone creature." She sounded like she was trying to convince herself.

Bee humphed.

"Bee's right," Amy said. "Bone creatures *had* feathers, once upon a time, when they were alive."

"So . . . ," said Theo. "These feathers came from a bone creature . . . that was alive?"

"Or one that just died recently," said Amy briskly. "It's clearly from one of the bone creatures the fairies fought off yesterday. And look: the fairy village barely survived the battle."

They stood and stared at the scene for a few minutes more. Then Bee said, "Joey, how does the story go from here?"

Everyone turned to Jojo, like she would know.

But Jojo wasn't going to get pulled into making up a fairy story. "The story doesn't go anywhere from here. It was *pretend*. Not real. There's no such thing as a bone creature."

"Then how do you explain the feathers?" said Amy. "And the blood?"

"Not blood. Mulberries," said Jojo.

Bee said, "It can't just be coincidence."

Theo nodded, as if he agreed—or at least wanted to agree—with the twins.

Suddenly Jojo realized what had happened. The answer was so obvious. "Theo came outside early this morning, before us, and did all this. To fool us."

"What?" said Theo.

"Why would he do that?" said Maisie. "You didn't, did you?"

"No!" said Theo.

"Well, that's that, then." Maisie looked pensively at the feather carnage.

Fine, not Theo. "Then it was the cat," said Jojo. "Eating a bird."

"It wasn't Fabio," said Bee in a small voice. "He would never."

"He would so," said Amy. "If he could. But he's too slow. And anyway, if he caught a bird, he'd never frost it with mulberries."

Everyone wandered off for a while after that, feeling grumpy, like they'd almost had a fight and then at the last minute avoided arguing—not by making up, but by pretending they were okay and saving the fight for later. It wasn't a great feeling. Amy and Bee went to the backyard and climbed trees; Maisie sat in the rocking chair with a book; and Theo and Jojo drew a chalk target on the side of the tree stump and threw rocks at it. Honestly, it wasn't the most exciting morning, especially considering there was a new kid to play with and a mystery to be solved.

Jojo felt especially grumpy because yesterday's secret was chewing at her brain like Fabio at a catnip mouse. It wouldn't let go.

The squirrel-sized person. Just like some fairies she'd once told a story about, with a long beard and muddy suspenders.

Not *a squirrel-sized person,* she reminded herself sternly. And not from a story. Just a squirrel, or a trick of the light. She tossed. Her rock landed early and rolled. No points.

Theo's rock hit the edge of the target. One point for him.

It wasn't only the not-a-fairy creature that bugged her. There was also this: the story she'd started telling last summer, the story about the bone creatures. She remembered it so clearly. They had found the dead bird when they were out walking with Grandma Nan. Jojo had started a story about the bird right after that. She remembered the lines that the twins liked to quote—and she remembered a lot more of the lines than they did. After all, she'd made them up. *Num-*

berless bone creatures flapped across the sky, their skeletal wings creaking, as they scouted for a fairy village to attack and pillage, which they did each week—until they found a grimy village of green fairies who lived on the edge of some wet, swampy land. Not a swamp, exactly—

Her rock veered off course again, sailing over the stump, and landed in the grass with a thunk.

Theo's next rock hit the target, dead center. Five points. Jojo was losing and she barely cared. She must be getting sick or something.

She'd never gotten around to finishing that story, and now the twins had taken it and added a queen sitting on a throne. The fairy queen hadn't been part of that original story—and there hadn't been a human queen in it either. Her story had only had the green fairies, grimy from the swampy land they lived in. The fairies . . . who looked like tiny, green, muddy people, some of them with green beards. . . .

Somehow, she told a story once, long ago, and then Bee and Amy added things from other stories, and now? It seemed like it was coming true. Or at least parts of it were. A muddy green fairy.

Stories becoming real wasn't supposed to happen. *Couldn't* happen.

Before Jojo's throwing turn could come again,

Maisie announced it was lunchtime. Theo's rock dinged off the edge of the stump, just nicking the target, for another point. He shrugged and very nicely didn't rub in that he was winning. "I have to leave after lunch," he said. "My uncle's taking me to the library, and then we're getting pizza for supper. Maybe I can look for your librarian when I'm at the library?"

"No!" said Jojo, dropping her last rock. "I mean, we . . . don't want to get her in trouble. And anyway, I think she's not working today."

"Pizza sounds yummy," said Bee, back with Amy from tree climbing. "I bet we'll have burnt hotdish again."

Theo looked a question.

"Leftovers from yesterday," explained Maisie.

While they ate lunch, they described the library to Theo so that he could find the best books right away.

"You don't have to leave yet, though?" said Bee. "Joey, tell a story first. About the fairies who left the gifts here."

She said "Joey" so nicely that Jojo almost didn't want to say something mean back. But she wasn't going to tell a story, especially not now that the stories seemed to be coming true in weird, unpredictable ways. She took her last bite of sandwich and answered with her mouth full. "I'm too busy for dorky fairy stories."

Bee's bottom lip wobbled.

Amy and Maisie both glared at Jojo.

"Fine," Maisie snapped. "*I'll* tell a story."

Jojo stayed on the porch because she wanted to hear what Maisie would say, not because she wanted to hear *fairy* stories. But she stood at the far end of the porch with a little pile of rocks and practiced throwing during the story, to show that she wasn't interested. She aimed for the back side of the stump, and she never hit it even once, because it was too far away.

I'll summarize what Maisie said, with just a few of the interruptions to give you the flavor of how it went. But you should know that the actual telling took a long time, and Jojo ran out of rocks long before Theo's uncle yelled that it was time to go.

There was a nation of fairies, said Maisie, that lived in a mansion with petals for carpet and shells for chairs and tables and beds—except the shell furniture was not hard and uncomfortable, but soft and cushy and perfect for sitting and sleeping. These fairies were mostly musicians and actors and made plays and musicals all the time. Old classics like *High School*

Musical and *Frozen*. And yes, they had gossamer wings. (There was another meandering discussion of *gossamer* at this point, and Theo didn't know what it meant either.)

Maisie continued: There was also a nation of fairies that lived in a wooden fort and fought off all the cats and caterpillars that attacked them, and they had a pet alligator in their moat who was unfriendly to their enemies but never bit the fairies and gave them rides on her back round and round the moat. These fairies made bows and arrows and shot things for a living. They won a lot of bow-and-arrow competitions all over the world.

And, of course, there was a nation of fairies whose queen had just died in a terrible bone creature attack, and they were waiting for a new queen or king to arrive, just like the prophecy foretold. The prophecy said—

"Jojo, what did the prophecy say?" Maisie asked. "In your story. I can't remember that part."

Sometime during the discussion of *gossamer*, Jojo had plunked down on the porch steps with her back to the sisters. She was listening but still pretending not to.

"Joeeeeeey," said Bee. "Maisie's asking you something."

"What was the prophecy?" Maisie said again.

Jojo kicked at the gravel at the bottom of the steps. "It was silly."

"We don't think so," said Maisie. "What was it?"

"It was about a human becoming queen."

"No," said Amy. "What *exactly* was it?"

Jojo remembered. She'd spent a lot of time on that story, and the prophecy she'd come up with was really cool. Or at least she'd thought so back when she thought fairies were cool. She shrugged, rolled her eyes, and cleared her throat. "'One of the people who is about to go through the doorway from human land to fairyland will become the new ruler, and the new ruler will save the fairies.'"

"I thought it was *queen*?" said Maisie. "Become the new queen."

Jojo remembered the words exactly. "I said *ruler*, actually, but we always thought it meant *queen*, so that it could be one of us."

"Right," said Maisie. "Now I remember. So—"

"Theo, five minutes!"

And that was the end of Maisie's story, which as you can see, had not gotten very far. Maisie was great at describing things but not very good at making things *happen*. There were no people in her story who were actually doing things. In fact, there wasn't—as

Amy was cruel enough to point out at this moment—any *story* in Maisie's story.

Maisie looked a little hurt, but then Theo said, "I liked it," and Maisie smiled. He added, "It is weird, though, that the carnage scene has all those new feathers and extra mulberries today." (Like the twins, he had started calling their garden *the carnage scene*.) "It seems like something bad happened last night. Really bad."

"We should write our fairies a note," said Bee, "and ask them what is the matter and if we can help." She looked worried.

"What?" said Jojo, turning to them. They should write a *note*? Really? "Fairies aren't—"

"—good readers all the time," said Maisie firmly. Over Bee's head she made a *Be quiet* face at Jojo, and Jojo glowered back.

Bee didn't seem to notice. "They'll read my letter," she said comfortably. "I know they will."

"Okay, but let me do the spelling," said Maisie.

As if spelling mattered when you were writing to imaginary creatures. Jojo rolled her eyes.

"Theo!" called his uncle again. "It's time!"

Maisie said, "Don't worry. We'll write the letter, but we won't do anything else, fairy-wise, without you. Not until tomorrow morning, when we'll all meet up again."

"Thanks!" said Theo. He ran off, turning to wave again at all of them before he got into his uncle's red car and rode away.

6

The Small Green Person

After Theo left with his uncle, the day crumpled. Jojo refused to sign the letter that Maisie and the twins wrote to the fairies—which Maisie put in her best handwriting and Amy drew blue hearts on. Bee taped a piece of candy to the card—it was linty and had been in her pocket for a long time, but on the other hand, it was butterscotch, and Bee thought the lint might make it taste even better to the fairies. Also it *sounded* good. Fuzzy butterscotch. After the note was complete, Bee added Jojo's name to it, along with a final heart, but Jojo didn't know that until she saw the finished card, when her sisters went to put it under the pine tree and she reluctantly followed them.

DEAR FAIRIES,

What is wrong? Did you lose the fight with the bone creatures?

Are you still alive? Are you wounded? Do you need help? What can we do? Here is a piece of candy, in case you need sugar energy.

Sincerely,

Maisie, Bee, and Amy

(And Theo, even though he is not here right now)

And Jojo

"You should put the note under a rock or it will blow away," said Jojo. Though maybe it was better if it did.

The sky was growing dark with clouds, and everything on the lawn suddenly looked dreary. Or menacing. Jojo wasn't sure which.

As Amy placed the note on the fairy throne, and Maisie put a rock on top of it, Jojo heard a belch. It was a quiet belch, but still a belch. It came from behind her.

"Who was that?" said Bee, looking around. "Who burped?"

"What?" said Maisie, straightening. Amy still knelt near the throne, brushing dirt off the note.

Jojo looked swiftly back. No one was near them—at least, no one their size. She studied the ground. There was something near that lilac bush. . . . A flash of greenish brown, and then—

Another burp, from under the bush where Jojo had seen the movement.

"That!" said Bee. She tugged Jojo's arm. "You heard it, right?"

Slowly Jojo shook her head. No.

"I heard it this time too," said Maisie.

"Me too!" Amy said, leaping up and running toward the lilacs. She circled the bush. "Nothing here. Unless this is maybe footprints?"

The girls looked. On the far side of the bush they found some scuffle marks, very small, like someone tiny had maybe run away quickly. Headed toward Theo's uncle's house, or maybe past it. Jojo remembered the muddy fairy from yesterday running behind the yellow house and into the woods—

Not a fairy.

Bee clapped her hands. "It's the fairies, I know it is! Oh! We need to get away from here so they can come out and get the letter." She grabbed Jojo's and Maisie's hands and tugged. "Come on!"

Amy ran ahead to the porch as Bee pulled Maisie and Jojo along.

Maisie shrugged, frowning. "We still have to stay outside."

A few drops of rain fell from the sky. And then more.

After the girls had left the letter under the rock in the twins' garden, the afternoon dragged on slowly. It rained, that dreary, misty kind of rain that isn't even fun to run around in because you never get properly soaked, you just get cold and damp; and anyway, the air turned chilly. The girls wrapped themselves in blankets and sat on the porch where it was dry. They left the letter where it was, since Bee and Amy's carnage scene was under the pine tree and the paper wouldn't get very wet.

Maisie spent the afternoon rereading one of her favorite books, laughing at all the funny parts and getting tears in her eyes before she even reached the sad section. Jojo tried to read too, but somehow it didn't feel like a reading kind of day. So she paced up and down the long, narrow porch. Amy and Bee played checkers with the chess set until Amy got mad about losing, and then the twins played fairy war with the chess pieces, with one side representing the bone creatures and the other side representing the fairies hoping for a human ruler to show up and save them; they played until Bee got tired of being the bone creatures. Then they played a game they made up where they lay on their backs and put their feet together up in the air to make a bridge. It was the dorkiest game ever.

"That is the dorkiest game ever," said Jojo as she stepped over Amy's head to pace to the other end of the porch.

Amy grabbed at Jojo's legs but missed.

"It's not," said Bee. "We make a bridge with one leg each"—she put one leg up, and Amy did too, making a perfect pointed bridge by putting their feet together—"and we make a castle with our other legs. And when we put them all together, they are called a camidge. You know. For *castle* and *bridge* squished together."

"Both sets of legs look like bridges," said Jojo. "Not a castle."

"It's a castle that is shaped like a bridge. It's a castle in disguise," said Amy, grabbing for Jojo's feet again as she returned, pacing.

Jojo veered and stepped over Bee's head instead. "And *camidge* doesn't make sense. That's not what you get when you squish the two words together. There's no *m* in *castle* or in *bridge*. It should be *cabidge* or something. *Cabbage*."

Maisie looked up from her book at Jojo. "You're mad because you're bored. Stop picking on the littles."

"Stop calling us 'the littles,'" said Amy.

Maisie was sitting with her back to the front yard, curled up in her blanket on a pillow, leaning against the porch railing. That is why she didn't see what happened next. But the other three, who were facing her and the lawn behind her, did.

Just over Maisie's shoulder, in the misty-gloomy yard, something moved.

Amy gasped.

"What *is* that?" asked Bee, pointing.

"What?" said Maisie, turning to look. But it was already gone.

It was something exactly like a tiny person, not much bigger than a squirrel, and it was running across the lawn carrying a piece of paper. It was the fairy Jojo had *not* seen yesterday morning and had definitely *not* heard belching or seen scurry behind the lilac bush just after lunch. The fairy was a pukey green color right down to its beard, and the white paper in its hand almost glowed in the half-light. The creature dashed behind the pine tree and disappeared from view.

Bee and Amy were already describing the fairy to Maisie—or trying to. They didn't agree on all the details. Bee thought it was the size of a small cat, and Amy thought more like the size of a big rat. Bee thought it looked bluish brown, and Amy thought it looked more brownish green. They did agree, however, that they'd seen a tiny person.

The twins leapt off the porch to explore around the pine tree, the two bigger girls following. Maisie whispered to Jojo, "What was it really?"

Jojo shrugged. "I didn't see anything." No way was she going to say. There had to be a better explanation for what she'd seen.

"I think it was a leprechaun," said Bee, stooping to search under the pine tree while her sister ran around it. "A very sick, damaged leprechaun."

Maisie caught up and put her hand on Bee's shoulder. "Leprechauns only live in Ireland, Bee-Bee."

"A gremlin, then," said Amy, puffing a little. "It was kind of hunchy and gremliny."

Jojo didn't think the creature had looked at all hunched, just small, but she didn't want to talk about it. "Whatever it was, it's gone now."

"Anyway," said Amy, "I guess it couldn't have been a fairy. Too big."

"And no gossamer wings," said Bee. "But it did have the green beard and the suspenders."

Jojo peeked under the pine tree at the twins' garden. The letter was gone.

The twins talked about the strange tiny person until supper. Even Maisie seemed interested. Of the four girls, only Jojo didn't want to talk about it. Yes, she used to make up stories about fairies and other magical creatures, but she never expected to *see* one in the yard. When Grandma Nan was sick, Jojo had imagined for a wild minute that the fairies might be real, and she'd asked them to make her grandma well again. And they hadn't. So even if they *were* real—*which they weren't*—Jojo didn't want to know them.

And yet she felt a small shiver of something down her spine. *What if?* What if they were real after all?

She paced the porch while the other three talked, and Bee and Amy got out paper and each drew pictures of how they remembered the little greenish creature.

At supper everyone was antsy. They'd agreed not to tell Mom about seeing a not-even-knee-high adult running through the yard. As Maisie said, that was the kind of thing that made parents nervous and unlikely to let you play in the front yard anymore.

But that meant they didn't know what to talk about, because the little stranger was on the front tip of every sister's brain, even Jojo's, and it was impossible to come up with other topics of conversation when there was a small pukey-green person perched on the front tip of your brain.

It turned out not to matter, though, because Mom was even moonier than yesterday. She shoveled leftover burnt hotdish into her mouth without noticing when the food slipped off the fork and she was taking bites of air. Her glasses were perched on the top of her head, and she squinted at her plate.

Finally Maisie said, "How are Willow and Vlag doing?"

Mom shuddered and looked at the girls like she was just seeing them for the first time that day. "You mean Vlad? They're shaping up nicely. I think they're actually going to fall in love."

She talks about them like they are real people, thought Jojo. "But can't you just *make* them fall in love? I mean, they're not real, right?"

Mom smiled and took a bite. A real bite this time, not an air bite. After she swallowed, she said, "They *feel* completely real when I'm writing them. It's as if me writing the story is what brings them to life. Like, because I told a story about them, they suddenly exist." Her face softened again, and she took an air bite, back in her daydream.

Jojo stared at her plate. The crusty black hotdish resembled the unexplored surface of a bleak planet. *If you tell a story,* Jojo thought, *you can make something real. That's what Mom means. If you tell a story, the thing you tell a story about might actually happen.*

Then she felt someone looking at her, and she glanced up from her plate. Maisie was giving her a worried look. And Jojo knew what she was thinking. What if the fairy stories she'd told a long time ago, the stories Bee and Amy remembered and had added to—what if they were turning real?

The next morning the girls all woke up super early, on their own, because no one needs an alarm clock to wake up in the summer. They had run out of milk, so they ate dry cereal, standing at the counter in the kitchen, quiet as mice so their mom wouldn't hear and wonder what they were doing up so early, and they all helped Maisie make the sandwiches and pack the cooler, and then they ran outside and around the house to the front porch, where Theo was already sitting on the porch steps.

There was so much to tell him. First, Bee and Amy reported that the letter was gone from under the rock. During the night that fact had seemed more and more important to them—and to Maisie, who explained how carefully she'd placed the rock on top of the note so it wouldn't blow away.

Then, of course, Amy and Bee told Theo all about the tiny green person they'd seen. Theo asked a lot of questions, which the twins couldn't answer, about who the tiny person was.

"Jojo saw too," said Bee helpfully.

Jojo could feel Theo looking at her for some answers, but she shook her head. "I'll put your lunch away."

Theo's lunch was a sandwich and an apple and a baggie of five store-bought cookies. Jojo stashed it all in the cooler, telling herself she was happy, because five cookies meant that Theo was planning to share.

"Cookies are so much better than carrots," she said brightly, turning to the group.

But they were gone.

Across the yard, under the pine tree, stood Maisie

and Theo and Bee and Amy. Only their legs were visible.

"See?" Amy was saying loudly. "The note is *still* gone." She sounded triumphant, as if she'd proved something.

"Because the gremlin took it," said Bee.

"Because a *squirrel* took it," called Jojo from the porch.

Theo bent way over, his head peeking out the bottom of the pine tree, to stare at Jojo. Upside down, his face looked round and confused. Then he crawled out and went over to her. "What did *you* see, exactly?" he asked.

The others came out too. Amy said, "We saw a fairy! Or maybe a gremlin."

"Like a tiny, tiny person," said Bee.

"Kind of muddy," added Amy.

"But only because of the rain," said Bee. "I'm sure they're not usually covered in mud."

Theo kept looking at Jojo, like he was waiting for her to answer. Finally she shrugged. "I didn't see anything," she said. It was a lie. And she knew it.

Amy and Bee both yelled at the same time that "there was too a tiny person" and Jojo was lying or maybe a bird brain (Amy said *bird brain*; Bee didn't). For a minute it seemed like their voices might get loud enough even for Mom to hear. But Maisie pulled both the little girls away from the house, toward the road, where they huddled and whispered with her.

Theo studied Jojo. "You didn't see *any*thing?"

"A squirrel, probably," said Jojo. "A muddy squirrel."

She'd seen a fairy. She knew she had, especially after having all night to think about it. She'd seen this same fairy several times now.

Which meant that fairies were real. Magic was real.

But she'd been thinking about it since she woke up. Real fairies were not better than pretend ones; they were worse. Because if fairies were real, then they hadn't helped her when she'd asked. They hadn't saved Grandma even though she'd begged them to.

After a break where Maisie took Amy and Bee for a short exploration in the backyard, and the twins found slugs and forgot (a little bit) how mad they were at Jojo, they all regrouped on the porch.

"What should we play now?" said Theo.

"We should look at the other fairy gardens," said Amy immediately. "To see if anything strange happened there."

"How about tag?" said Maisie.

"After," said Bee.

Theo said slowly, "I do want to see the gardens again before they get wrecked. It's supposed to storm tonight."

They all looked at Jojo.

"Fine," said Jojo in her snottiest voice. "Let's look one more time before the rain destroys them. And then we can be done with this baby game."

Amy said, "You're mean."

Bee sniffed loudly.

Jojo felt a little bit guilty. "Fine," she said in a slightly nicer voice. "Let's look."

They stopped at the porch to eat the cookies first, for fortification, and then went back out to inspect the gardens.

Maisie's and Jojo's looked exactly the same as yesterday—which was odd, since they'd gotten rained on all yesterday afternoon. In Maisie's mansion, the carpet of rose petals looked perfect and fresh, and at Jojo's moat, the murky moat water still came right up to the alligator rock's glaring eyes and no farther.

Theo studied Maisie's mansion thoughtfully. "There's a rosebush way back in the woods behind my house," he said. He meant his uncle's house. And he meant the empty lots behind the house, which were overrun with trees and had a small creek running through them. The girls always called it the woods too. "I think someone planted roses a long time ago, maybe when there was a house back there."

"We never saw a rosebush," said Maisie. "Or a house." She sounded slightly accusing.

"There's no house anymore. But the rosebush is there, up a little hill," said Theo. "My uncle and I saw it on our walk last night. It's just a little way past the fairy door. Hey, did you put that door there?"

"We did!" said Maisie. Which was not *quite* true, as Jojo hadn't helped. Maisie and Amy and Bee had made the door during the winter, and then, when spring came, they'd hunted for the perfect tree and nailed it to the trunk, all while Jojo glowered and refused to join in. She hadn't even gone to the woods with them to install the door. She'd stayed home with Mom that day—Mom wasn't on deadline then—and helped her make muffins, even though normally Jojo didn't like baking because it was too fussy. But in this case, it was something real and they'd get muffins out of it, unlike a fairy door, which wouldn't give them anything.

She'd seen her sisters painting the fairy door, though, and heard them talking about it. It was bright blue, from leftover paint in a paint-by-number set of Maisie's, and it was small, about the size a squirrel might fit through if it were a real door. But it wasn't a real door. It was just scraps of wood, painted and then nailed to the bottom of a tree. And, as the three girls told Mom later, they had laid pretty rocks around it and even planted flowers with a packet of seeds they'd found in the basement.

They hadn't talked about the fairy door in a while, Jojo realized. At least not when she was around.

"Did the flowers grow?" asked Maisie.

Theo said, "The daisies? They're huge."

Amy clapped. "We should go look! I bet it's beautiful."

"Can we go now? Instead of tag?" Bee asked Maisie, as if Maisie were in charge.

"We agreed on tag," said Jojo. "Not woods."

"We can change our minds," said Amy. She was still mad about earlier. Jojo could tell.

"Well . . . ," said Maisie. "We could. . . ."

Jojo felt herself getting full of steam, like a teakettle about to shriek. She didn't *want* to go to the woods and find a dopey fairy door. She didn't want fairies. She didn't want to think about the magical stories she and Grandma Nan used to tell, and most of all, she didn't want to think about Grandma Nan being gone. "I want to play *tag*," she said. "No one ever listens to me, and *I want tag!*" Her voice was yelling now.

She kicked down her fort, scattering sticks everywhere, and stomped through Maisie's mansion petals. Her eyes were stinging, but not because she was sad. No, she was *mad*. No one ever listened to her or played the games she wanted. Well, fine. She made the worst, meanest face she could make and turned back to them, her hands in fists. Her sisters and Theo all stood frozen next to the destroyed fort and mansion, staring at her like they didn't even know who she was.

"I . . . am . . . going . . . back . . . to . . . the . . . porch." With her mean face on, she said each word slow and loud. Like she was biting it off a string and spitting it on the ground. "And . . . I . . . am . . . playing . . . tag. *By myself.*" Then she walked toward the porch. She was shaking.

Behind her, Theo said, "Tag?" like he didn't understand what the word meant. "Jojo, wait. . . ."

He was following her. She walked faster, then ran. She needed to get away from everyone. The porch—

She stopped short. Her heart pounded. There. On the porch. *No.*

Theo ran into her from behind, and they both almost fell.

Maisie said, "What is it?" and she and Bee and Amy joined them.

It was—

It was—

Lying on the porch was a greenish fairy, filthy and sound asleep, snoring quite loudly, clutching a crumpled note in its hand.

7

Roland

Maisie and Theo were shocked to see a squirrel-sized greenish person sleeping on the porch. Amy and Bee were ecstatic—and a little smug, given that they'd known fairies were real even when Jojo said they weren't.

Jojo was neither shocked nor ecstatic (nor smug), because she had known, deep down, that she'd seen what she'd seen, even though she'd decided she was wrong—the way she might have, in the old days, looked at a dark gray sky right before an outdoor birthday party and known that rain was coming but still tried to believe that, *nonono*, the sun would come out any minute and the party would *not* have to end just before the scavenger hunt, with everyone trooping indoors to eat cake and drink punch while squishing into a too-small kitchen, trying not to spill.

Deep down she'd always known she'd seen something real. Maybe not a fairy like in books or movies. But this—this *someone*, snoozing on their porch, *did* look like the fairies in some of Jojo's old made-up stories: Squat and muddy. And with the long green beard and the suspenders. Definitely like something magical.

What she had really hoped was that the creature would disappear and not come back.

"Wow," said Theo. "Just . . . wow."

"It's even green," whispered Bee. "Like we said."

"Like *I* said," whispered Amy.

The fairy was definitely green*ish*. Brownish green, really: covered from head to toe in mud. It didn't smell great; in fact, it smelled kind of like throw-up. And its face? The kids peered closely. Jojo thought it didn't look entirely human—more rodentish, with a twitchy nose and sharp teeth. (It was snoring with its mouth open.)

The tiny creature opened its eyes.

No one said anything. They all held their breath.

The tiny person sat up, rubbing its eyes and stretching. Then it nodded to the kids.

"You look just like the boy fairies that Jojo invented that one time," gasped Bee. "The ones with the green beards and the overalls."

"And the mud," added Amy.

"I am in fact a boy fairy," said the fairy. He put his hand over his heart as if to swear he was telling the truth.

"How . . . how do you do?" breathed Maisie, backing up a step.

He jabbed the note up toward them. "I got your scrip."

Carefully Theo reached forward and took the note. It was smeared from the rain but still readable. The candy they'd taped to it was gone. There was a small, muddy handprint where the green man had been holding it.

The green man stood on the blanket. He wasn't even as tall as their knees. "Cap'n Tom says, 'Thank you and yes.'"

"Captain Tom?" said Maisie.

"Our leader."

"Your leader's name is Tom?" Jojo felt like everything was moving too fast; or maybe she didn't understand English.

"No. *Cap'n Tom* means *leader*. Peppercorn is our Cap'n Tom's name. Meaning our leader." The visitor rolled his eyes as he spoke, like he couldn't believe he was explaining something so simple. When he finished, he plopped back down and closed his eyes and started snoring again.

He had to be pretending.

"Wait a minute," said Maisie. "What do you mean, 'Thank you and yes'? Why did you take our note that we wrote to the fairies?"

"And who is this Peppercorn person?" asked Theo.

The little man snored louder. Fabio wove between Theo's and the girls' legs and approached the snoring visitor, then nudged him with his cat nose and tickly whiskers and finally patted him with his paw as if to check if he was dead. The little man opened his eyes again. But he didn't sit up this time. He glared at them from where he was lying on Amy's blanket—which was the softest, though not, anymore, the cleanest.

"First of all, I filched the scrip because it was *addressed* to my people. Not to the fort fairies or the castle fairies, but to *us*. You left it in our historical battlefield re-creation."

"Your . . . what?" said Jojo.

"Our historical battlefield. Re-creation of the battle of 1692—in your time, that's just a couple of days ago. It's dab work, that battlefield. Nice job."

"You mean—" said Amy.

"—that our fairy garden is *real*?" said Bee in a delighted voice.

"I don't know nothing about a garden," the little man said, scrunching up his nose. "But the historical battlefield re-creation is banging."

"Banging is . . . good?" said Amy.

"So the part about the queen dying . . . ?" said Bee.

"She were offed by bone creatures, yes. Why're you asking me? You must ken the history, since you made the battlefield."

"Right . . . ," said Maisie. She sounded like she was dreaming.

Jojo felt a little bit like she was listening to a conversation underwater: mouths were moving, but nothing made sense. The creature was claiming that Amy and Bee had somehow made a *real* replica of a war that his people had lived through? With the mulberries and the grass throw-up and the bird skull? And all of it made up from patched-together stories she'd once told?

Theo cleared his throat. "Maybe we can start with names. I'm Theo." He quickly introduced the sisters. "What's your name? You're . . . a fairy? Or . . . something?"

"Finally," said the creature. "A dandyprat with manners. I'm Roland, one of the fairies of the fen."

Roland? Jojo shook her head. That wasn't a fairy name from any of her stories.

"Fairies of the fen?" said Theo.

"We kip in swamps and bogs and fens, and we sport ourselves in mold and moss. . . . Oh, I see." He looked around at them all, his lip curled in disgust. "You want the prissy nickum-poop *mansion* fairies with their little gossamer wings, and maybe also the bastinading *fort* fairies, those that curse their enemies. Not the grungy, hardworking fen fairies who kip in the mud. We ain't *good* enough for you."

"Are . . . the gossamer-winged fairies real too?" asked Maisie in a hopeful voice. "And are they going to visit?"

Roland snorted. The snorting made him sneeze, and he sneezed several times, covering his mouth with Amy's blanket and wiping his nose on it. Then he stood up with his muddy bare feet (also on Amy's blanket) and said, "You queried if we need help. Us, the fen fairies. And we do. You going to back out now?"

Everyone was quiet for a few seconds. Jojo could smell Roland from where she stood, several feet away from him, and she wondered if a group of a dozen fen fairies together would smell a dozen times stronger. Old vomit and moldy swamp.

Theo said, "No, we're not going to back out. We'll help."

Maisie said, "Of course we will!"

Amy nodded, and so did Bee, who was sucking on two fingers like she used to do when she was a baby.

No one seemed to notice that Jojo didn't answer.

"What is it," asked Maisie, "that you need us to do?"

The Prophecy

Before Roland could explain what the fairies needed, he wanted food. "The candy was no help. Candy won't fill up a gut-foundered belly. Don't you scatterbrats know that?"

So they decided to have lunch even though it was barely past breakfast time. Maisie thought for a moment and then said, "Rules can be broken in true emergencies. We'll sneak in and make more sandwiches later. Quietly." Which meant she took the situation very seriously.

Mostly, the five kids eating early lunch was them sitting on the porch watching Roland eat early lunch, though they did share an apple between them. Roland ate all the sandwiches and four of the five apples, and somehow when he was done, his round belly didn't look any bigger than it had when he started.

He patted his stomach after his last bite. "Finally, I don't feel starved—barely." And he belched loudly.

"*Excuse* me," said Maisie. She was used to telling Jojo and the twins how to be polite.

"Did you fart?" asked Roland. "You're excused. Better out than in. And better out loudly than quietly, am I right?"

Maisie frowned. "You're not at all what we expected in a fairy."

"No gossamer wings," said Bee sadly. She scooted next to Roland, who didn't seem to mind.

"Nope. Those duds are always ripping," said Roland. "Glad not to be stuck with that tripe."

"Anyway," said Jojo, who could see that Maisie was about to explain how beautiful gossamer wings were (at least in stories), "you were going to tell us about what we can do to help?" She narrowed her eyes. "If we decide to help you."

"Of course we will!" said Bee. She patted Roland's head.

Roland snapped his small, sharp teeth at Bee. "I'm a grown fairy. No patting." Then he studied Jojo for a minute, staring at her so hard, she felt like he was reading her mind.

"What?" she said, shifting on the blanket she was sharing with Theo. She didn't like feeling like he could read her mind. Not right now, anyway.

"I'm not sure why you're bothered at me, mollie, but if you think I did wrong by you, or you think my kinsfolk did, I can promise you that we never laid eyes on you until yesterday—well, day before yesterday, your time. The yesterday when I found your letter, and the day before when I scarfed that plate of food you left for us." (Amy and Bee gasped.) "Before that, we knew a bit about you, because in *our* stories you made us up, way back when. But we never actually *happened* on you; most of us thought you weren't real. So if you're grudging because the fairies took a whack at you sometime, it was some other fairies what done it, not us." He paused. "Probably the ruffians with the gossamer wings."

"Why do you say that?" asked Maisie.

"They're not as sweet as they look, the gossamer-wing fairies."

Jojo studied Roland. His people were magical; surely they didn't need help from a bunch of kids. What was he *really* here for?

Roland was now picking his nose, and Maisie dug

in her pocket and handed him a Kleenex. "Got a bug in there," he muttered, excavating with the tissue.

"Are you . . . done?" asked Maisie.

"Done with me nose!" said Roland. "But not done jawing at you." He gave the wadded tissue back to Maisie, who grimaced and took it by a corner. "We really do need your help, seeing as how you're supposed to save us." He paused to look them each in the eye. "And we're willing to give you something in trade. Grant a wish. Magical."

"A magic wish?" said Jojo. Her heart suddenly felt big inside her chest, like she'd just run a long way very fast. A magic wish . . .

Theo took a deep breath, eyes wide.

Bee and Amy shrieked and clapped their hands.

Maisie stuffed the tissue in her shorts pocket, hygiene concerns forgotten. "A wish? Like in fairy tales? Like, we could be princesses, or—"

"Not at all like fairy tales," said Roland. "In fairy tales, humans make reckless wishes and then things go all out of kilter. Have you not noticed? They turn to frogs, things like that. But we fen fairies will grant a wish without that kind of overboard nonsense. A wish within reason; there are some jigs we just can't dance. But there's a lot of magic we *can* do. I, for example, can eat almost any bug or rotted thing without getting sick. I can burrow into the muck in the flash of an eye. Loads of other things too."

"But . . . we *could* be princesses?" said Maisie. She glanced at Theo and Jojo. "As an example."

"You could be princesses for an afternoon."

"Would we have to comb our hair?" asked Bee. "Because then I vote no."

"Eating bugs would be fun," said Amy, sliding closer to Roland on her blanket.

Maisie said, "We'll have to take a vote."

"*After* you help us," said Roland. "We don't grant wishes in advance. And remember: a reasonable wish, something smallish. No bibbidi-bobbidi-boo that makes you the new princess of Tasmania"—he looked at Maisie—"and no shiny airplanes to fly you to an arctic expedition"—his glance slid across Theo—"and no giant insect rattling up a skyscraper, trying to take over the world"—his eyes flitted to the twins. "And especially no tricky supernatural jigs, like . . . well, like bringing someone back from the dead. Or anything like that." He did not look at anyone when he said this last bit. "Can't do it, won't try."

Jojo hadn't even been thinking about that kind of a wish. But now she was. Was Roland trying to make her think about Grandma Nan and how much she missed her?

She wasn't going to think about it.

But of course, now she *was*.

Which made her feel angry.

Then Roland burped, and his voice turned hearty again. "But a short-term, smallish magic wish, that we can do. Want to fly around the yard? Or maybe you want to nip along as a squirrel for an afternoon. Or . . ." He trailed off, scratching his nose.

Maisie took a deep breath. "We'll think of something. Meanwhile, what do you need from us?"

"Right," said Jojo, standing up. Action was better than thinking. "What do we need to do?"

Bee jumped up too, Amy bobbing next to her. "We'll help you, Roly."

"Roland, not Roly. Never Roly. Come with me and I'll show you."

"Where?" asked Theo.

"When?" asked Maisie.

"Now, and to fen fairyland. Let's lope."

Now wasn't exactly *now*. The kids would be gone awhile, so they needed to bring a lunch—which meant they needed to make a new one. And Maisie refused to go inside to make more lunches, she announced, until Roland explained what fen fairyland was like, and where it was, and why they needed to go there, and if her little sisters would be safe there, and—well, she had a million worried questions.

Roland put his hand up to stop her. He guessed he had a few minutes to explain. Everyone who was standing sat back down on the porch, on the pillows and blankets, and listened to Roland's story. Even Jojo couldn't help listening, especially now that she knew fairies could do magic and that she and the others would get a wish when this was all over.

Roland's story went like this (I'm summarizing, because unless you know his way of speaking, Roland is a little hard to understand sometimes, and the kids had to keep pausing to ask him to explain his strange-to-them words):

There are many fairylands, because they spring into existence as soon as a story is told about them. So, yes, there was a fort fairyland like Jojo had created, and a mansion fairyland like Maisie had built. (Jojo squirmed, knowing that she hadn't really built her fort for fairies; Maisie sighed in longing for mansion fairyland.) Many of the fairylands were crammed with little glittering Tinker Bell types who spoke in high voices and died if people didn't believe in them. Roland didn't have much good to say about these fairylands, except that they served delicious cakes there, and nectar drinks. But you had to put up with the glittering, smug, terrible happiness of the Tinker Bells to get a bite of cake, and he didn't think that was worth it.

If these fancy fairylands existed just because people told stories about them, then it logically followed that there was also a fairyland that Jojo (and her sisters) had told stories about, a fairyland in which the fairies had just fought off a bunch of bone creatures, and their queen had been killed, and they were awaiting the arrival of human help, as the prophecy had foretold. (Though Roland said "fore-telled," the way Bee and Amy did.)

"I don't get it," said Jojo. "I—we—made that world up. And I never even came up with a good end to the story."

"Humbug!" said Roland. (He said *humbug* just as if it were a curse word. Bee shivered.) "Humbug and blast it! We don't want an *end* to the story! Blech! We just want your assistance. A long time ago you cre-ated us, and now, in this contract"—he held up the paper—"you offered to help us; so I was sent to col-lect you. It's that simple."

"But," said Jojo, "I never told a story about *you*, and neither did my sisters. I mean, I never created someone called Roland. Did any of you?" She looked around at her sisters and at Theo. They all shook their heads no.

The squashy fairy frowned. "Don't you ken what I just said? You—all of you, but mostly you, Jojo—you made up stories about fairyland, and everything you told came real. That's a fact. But then, once we became real, we started living our own lives, and doing things by our own choices, because why wouldn't we? I mean, you don't expect us to just couch it, do you? And wait for you to think on us again?"

"I guess not," said Jojo slowly.

"So to continue the tale: right soon, the bone creatures showed up. You made them up too, you know. Like a simkin. Did you never think they'd try to mill us?"

"I didn't really ... think ... ," said Jojo.

Roland snorted.

Bee, who was sitting next to Jojo, took her hand and patted it.

"You didn't *think*." The small green fairy put his hands on his hips and glared around the circle at all of them. "You're all simkins. The bone creatures attacked us and we had to fisticuff them away. With great loss of life and blood. And then, finally, somehow these two"—he gestured at Bee and Amy— "figured that battle out and built a historical replica of it."

"I think it's called a diorama," said Theo. "I saw

one at a museum once, with my—with my mom." His face turned funny for a second and then back to normal.

"And *you* made up a prophecy," said Roland to Jojo, as if Theo hadn't spoken at all. "After the recent battle, one of our fairies found the prophecy scraped into a rock in the fen, and it foretelled"— he sounded a bit disgusted now—"the human who would save us."

Maisie, sitting on the other side of Jojo, murmured, "The prophecy from a long time ago? The one you recited for me yesterday when I asked you?"

Dazed, Jojo nodded. She felt like all she could do right now was nod. This wasn't how stories were supposed to work. You didn't make up a story and then it became true and then it also started grabbing things from other stories and then put them all together and wrote itself. And the people in the story didn't just start living their own lives when you looked away from them. Stories didn't *work* that way.

She must have said the last sentence out loud, because Roland turned to her and said, "But sometimes they do. That's the way with stories sometimes."

Theo cleared his throat. "So, what can we do?"

"We ken—no, we *hope*—that one of you is the

human from the prophecy. The one who can save us and become our new queen." He gestured to Theo. "Or, I guess, king?"

Theo nodded.

"And then what?" said Jojo. She had a sinking feeling.

"And then stay in fairyland to rule us. It's not a hard job, don't worry. Just sitting on the throne and looking dandy. And fighting off the bone creatures."

"Stay in fairyland?" asked Maisie faintly.

"Fight off bone creatures?" murmured Theo.

"Why is this so hard to understand? *You* made the prophecy up!" Roland gestured to all of them. "It's not like we begged for a human queen. 'Ohhh, *please*, can we be ruled by a human?' No, we did not yelp that. But now it's the blasted prophecy, and *you wrote it*, so you better live up to it."

"Stay in fairyland and fight off the bone creatures," said Jojo, "and then you give us a magical wish." It was a question, but it sounded like a regular sentence. Stay in fairyland and fight monsters, get something magical. Like a trade. She knew she couldn't have her grandma back—knew it before Roland had said he couldn't bring things back to life, because she wasn't a baby anymore and she knew how the world worked—but maybe something else, something that would fix how miserable she felt? She didn't know what, but—

"Yep, that's the ticket," Roland said. "You got it now." He belched.

9

Fen Fairyland

Well, what was there to do but make more sandwiches and go to fairyland? I mean, really, given all the kids knew now about the fairies' plight—and how much of it was their own fault—they *had* to go. The throne was unfilled and the fen people were in danger. "The bone creatures'll be back," said Roland. "They've not piked off for good. And then . . ." He drew his finger in a line across his neck and made a snicking sound. "Then we're milled."

After Maisie had snuck back into the house and quietly remade the sandwiches, they set off.

But first they had to lock Fabio inside, because

now he suddenly decided he was awake and full of energy, and he kept trying to follow them; and everyone knows you don't bring a cat into fairyland. After Jojo caught him, Maisie stuffed him in the house and shut the back door firmly. And *then* they set off, Fabio now glaring at them murderously from the front window, which, like the front door and unlike all the basement and second-floor windows, did not open.

At first Roland said he needed to blindfold all the kids so they would never be able to find the entrance back on their own, but Amy immediately guessed where the entrance was: it was the fairy door that they'd built into the tree in the woods. Then Roland sulked and said there was no use in blindfolding them or even taking them anywhere. So they all said he could blindfold them anyway if it would make him happy, and that promise cheered him up, though when he did it (tying a smelly, muddy pocket handkerchief around each of their faces), they tripped and fell as he tried to lead them across the yard, so he gave up and let them walk with the handkerchiefs around their necks if they promised to *pretend* they were blindfolded.

They trailed across the deserted road, around Theo's uncle's house, and into the backyard. Roland went first, holding one end of Theo's belt, with Jojo right behind, holding the other end, so that Roland could lead her. The rest of the kids followed Roland and Jojo, holding hands in a line that ended with Maisie and the lunch cooler.

"I wonder where we are going," said Bee loudly. "I can't see anything."

"It smells piney, like maybe the woods," said Theo.

"I feel the sun on my face, so we must be heading north," said Amy. (She did not know her directions.)

Maisie, who was lugging the food, didn't say anything; and Jojo, who was thinking many thoughts, didn't say anything either.

"Come along, and don't trip over these rocks you can't eyeball," said Roland.

Her mind elsewhere, Jojo stumbled.

"Nice work," whispered Theo from behind her. "That seemed almost real."

When Jojo and her sisters and Theo did get to the fairy door, Roland told them they could take their blindfolds off, so they removed the kerchiefs from around their necks and gave them back to him. He stuffed all of them into a tiny pocket in his pants, and somehow they all fit.

The daisies that Maisie, Bee, and Amy had planted

that spring were in full bloom around the fairy door, which was a little strange, since it was deeply shady under the tree. (After they had planted the daisies, Maisie had read aloud the back of the packet and they had realized they should have planted them somewhere sunny.) Little stones ringed the tree like the boundary of a yard. The door itself was a festive bright blue.

"Shake your shambles! Through we go!" said Roland, his hand on the oversized nail the three sisters had bent to look like a handle.

"Hold on," said Theo, refastening his belt. "We can't fit through that door."

"The cooler won't fit either," said Maisie.

"Have faith in fairy magic," said Roland. He hacked and then spit off to the side. His spit was greenish.

Maisie blinked a long blink and turned her face away, shuddering.

Roland ignored her squeamishness. "Hike behind me. Close your goggles if you have to. You know: if you're scared." He glared at them as if to say, *Anyone who needs to close their eyes is a baby.*

"I'm not scared," said Amy. Bee nodded.

"Just grab the handle," Roland said, "and open the door, and leg it through"—which he did, closing the door behind him as he disappeared into fairyland.

The five kids stared at the door and at one another.

"It . . . opened—didn't it?" said Amy. "And he went through?"

Jojo nodded slowly. Fairy magic must be powerful.

"Did you build the door to open?" asked Theo.

Maisie shook her head no. "It's just boards painted blue and nailed to the tree."

"But how did he . . ." Theo shook his head. "Okay, then. I'll go next, and you girls follow." He walked bravely up to the little door, crouched low to the ground, and studied it. His hand moved toward the bent nail, but he couldn't seem to make himself grab it. "I'm not sure. . . ."

"I'll go," said Jojo. She wanted to test out the magic. "But you all better follow. Maisie goes last." She knew that Maisie would make sure everyone else got through, and then she'd go through herself because she wouldn't be able to bear being left behind.

Theo stood and backed away, and Jojo walked up to the door, bent down, and without giving herself a chance to think, grabbed the handle—

And then suddenly—

Who knew how—

The door was big enough for her to walk through—

And the handle was a real handle, not just a nail—

And she pulled the door open—

And on the other side lay a whole sunny-bright world, and she stepped through, and she was in fairyland.

10

On the Fen

The other kids came through the door in exactly the order that Jojo would have predicted if she'd thought about it: Amy and Bee appeared next, holding hands (Amy in the lead); then Theo; and finally Maisie, with the cooler of food, looking both slightly annoyed at almost being left behind and relieved to see that everyone was okay.

Jojo spread her arms out to fairyland. For once, she couldn't think of any words to say.

Neither could anyone else, so they all stood and stared.

It wasn't that the world looked *that* different from

their own: trees and flowers and grass and stuff like that. It was that their perspectives had changed so much. As on the home side of the door, there were daisies here, but now they were as tall as Jojo. One flower opened directly behind Theo; the petals flared out around his head like white sunbeams, his head the sun.

"How . . . did everything . . . get so big?" Jojo finally asked.

Amy giggled. "You're joking, right?"

Jojo tore her eyes away from the world to look at Amy. Amy looked exactly the same as always. All of them did. It was just that the rest of the world had grown so much. "What do you mean?"

Maisie said, "You couldn't see it, because you were the first of us to go through. And when you grabbed the door handle, it *felt* like the door got bigger."

"But really you got smaller," said Theo. "You shrank, and then you went through."

"This world isn't bigger than ours," said Maisie. "We're just really, really small."

"Fairy size," said Bee. "Or at least, Roland size. Maybe smaller than him, since he's a grown-up." She paused. "Isn't he?"

"Where *is* he, anyway?" said Maisie.

Theo looked around. "I'm sure he's nearby. . . ."

They stared around at this new world, a little

afraid to venture out now that they were roughly the size of a squirrel (or smaller, since Roland was squirrel sized). The daisy smell, so faint in the human world, was strong and pungent. A fist-sized bumblebee lumbered past, and they all jumped back. She rolled dozens of her hundred eyes at them but didn't pause on her jolting trek among the flowers.

Downslope from the oak tree lay a path of some kind, winding along like a dusty brown river. Jojo started toward it, and the rest followed, wondering where the path might lead.

But even reaching the path was an adventure. Where their tree stood at the top of a hill, the grass was short, not even up to their waists. Outside the tree's shade, however, the grass shot up taller than their heads and became difficult to wade through: every bump in the ground became a knee-high hill they had to scramble over, and they couldn't see the path ahead of them anymore. With the big tree towering behind them, they struggled downhill and hoped they were still heading in the right direction. Finally they parted the grasses to find a wide ditch filled with enormously tall cattails. They scrambled down the ditch and up the other side, gingerly stepping across the mud at the bottom of the trench, holding on to cattail stems for support and hoping not to fall in.

Luckily, no one sank deeper than their knees, and no one lost shoes or sandals to the muck, though Bee had a close call. They were all panting as they climbed out of the ditch and emerged on the path.

And there, in front of them, lay Roland, on his back on the edge of the dirt road, eating a mulberry almost as big as his hands, juice running down the sides of his face and into his greenish hair. He sat up. "Welcome! I thought you'd kicked it. What took so long?"

Now that they were roughly Roland's size, he looked even dirtier than he had when he was small and they were large. His green face was covered in layers of mud, like an archeological dig, and his hair was greasy, stalks of grass mashed into it on one side. And he sported purple-red streaks in his hair from the mulberry—though that addition looked pretty good. Jojo wondered how purple-red streaks would look in her own hair.

Roland stood up and blew out his lips like he was tired of waiting. He had terribly bad breath.

Bee coughed. "Do you ever brush your teeth?" Maisie elbowed her, but Jojo had been thinking the same thing.

"Brush my teeth?" asked Roland, as if he'd never heard of such an idea. "I brush my hair, once per year before Mud Days. Is that what you mean?" He grinned with his mouth open. Jojo wasn't sure, but it was possible that a gnat flew out.

"What . . . kind of food . . . do you usually eat?" asked Maisie faintly. She looked like she was holding her breath.

"Mulberries, of course," said Roland, wiping his face with his arm. "That's what our blood is made of."

"It *is*?"

"Well, sure. Remember the totally accurate historical re-creation in your yard? Mulberry blood."

They all nodded.

"And we nosh on mud and grass, usually mixed with slugs to make it tasty. Again, the historical replication was excellent: the green stuff is exactly what our throw-up looks like. Sometimes with mulberries mixed up in it too."

"Ah," said Theo, gagging a little. "Right."

"But fairies like to eat human treats too," he said. "Like, say, whatever is in the cooler. We wouldn't say no to that."

"That's for lunch," said Maisie, shoving the cooler (which fortunately had shrunk to the right size) behind her back. She wasn't going to run home and make sandwiches again. "But I packed enough to share, *when* it's lunchtime."

There was a brief, awkward silence.

"So," said Jojo, "what's the plan? We're here. What are we supposed to do now? I mean . . . the queen thing." She couldn't stay here forever, not even to be a queen, and neither could her sisters, and she was pretty sure Theo wouldn't be able to stay either. But they could figure that part out later. Right now they just needed to do enough so that the fairies would give them some magic.

Suddenly, somewhere behind them, in the direction of the giant tree, Jojo heard a noise.

"What was that?" asked Maisie.

Bee and Amy had wandered a few feet away, had found a half-blown cattail lying on the path, and were now draping themselves in cotton. Theo was studying the sky, turning slowly as he did. None of them noticed the sound. Roland frowned, though; he'd heard the noise too.

It had sounded like a door opening and shutting again. None of them could see the fairy door through the tall grass; they could see only the top of the oak tree far off up the hill.

"It ain't someone coming through *our* door," said Roland. "Can't be. We made the magic to work only for you: you people what made the fairy gardens. No one else can get through."

Jojo said, "Should we be worried?"

"Yes, I think we should," Theo answered, even though Jojo hadn't been talking to him and he hadn't been paying attention to her and Roland and Maisie. He was still studying the sky, and now he pointed. "We should probably worry. Because isn't that—I mean, I've never seen one before in real life, but isn't that a bone creature?"

And sure enough, low on the horizon ahead of them, a single skeletal bird flapped and wheeled across the blue blue sky.

11

Peppercorn and Prophecies

Luckily, fen fairyland lay in the opposite direction of the skeleton bird that soared in the sky. So the kids turned their backs on the bone creature—which did not feel comfortable at all—and followed Roland away from it. Because Maisie refused to be the last person in line anymore, Jojo volunteered. The bird thing was creepy, after all, but as Jojo knew from her own story about it, it was only robin sized. Not that big. She remembered finding the baby bird on that walk with Grandma Nan, seeing its fragile body, and wondering if all birds were so delicate under their feathers. And if people were like that too, if

their souls—or whatever was deep inside them—
were maybe thin and fragile and symmetrical like the
bones of a bird.

And then, later that day, she'd started telling a
story about bone creatures, a horror story meant to
scare her sisters just enough to make their eyes get
big, but not enough to give them nightmares. And
she'd never wondered where that story might lead
or what power it might have. As she and her sisters
and Theo and Roland walked through fairyland now,
she could feel the bone creature flying in the sky far
behind her, though she refused to stop and look.

And *then* she remembered that even though the
monster was only the size of a robin, she herself was
now also about the size of a robin. She walked a little
faster.

Roland was at the front of the line with Amy and
Bee behind him, oohing and aahing over every enormous plant and insect. Theo carried the lunch cooler.
Maisie walked just in front of Jojo, probably feeling
a little guilty that she'd consigned her sister to the
most dangerous end of the line. But Jojo didn't mind,
if only she could stop thinking about bone birds and
how big they were compared with her.

After walking for some time, they all paused to
study a praying mantis poised on a nearby bush. The

insect seemed menacing now, more than she ever would have when the kids were regular-sized humans, and she flicked her prayer hands at them; Jojo imagined her eating her husband's head off, which is what praying mantises do, as Jojo knew, because she'd read it in a book. But now this fact seemed less *interesting* and more *terrifying*. She sped up to walk right behind Maisie.

They paused several more times, to look at a few more insects and a field mouse—and a squirrel, who thankfully ignored them, because they were so small, it could easily have beaten them up—and eventually, finally, they came to the edge of a vast, swampy land. Small hills jutted up, covered with clumps of grass and short flowers, and lots and lots of puddles lay between the clumps, puddles with a whitish look to them. The ground everywhere looked wet.

"This is a marsh, right?" said Theo. "Or a bog?" He sounded like someone who'd read a book about wetlands but hadn't ever seen one in real life.

Roland snorted loudly. "Simkin. We're called *fen* fairies."

"Oh! It's a *fen!*" shouted Amy.

"Is that a kind of marsh?" Theo asked.

"Better. Rarer. Magicaler. In a fen the water oozes up out of the ground; water's always creeping skyward. In the winter she makes ice domes you can slide on, and in the summer her ground is a wet sponge. A fen is perfect."

"It must be hard to build houses here," said Maisie. "And stay dry." She shook her head at her already-muddy shoes.

Roland sputtered, "Who wants to build houses and stay dry? We couch right on the ground, or sometimes *in* it. Keeps us well watered and hale."

Jojo recalled that Bee and Amy hadn't built a home of any kind in their historical replica.

But they *had* built a twig seat for the fairy queen.

As if he'd read her mind, Roland said, "The throne is yonder."

They followed Roland through the marsh—the fen, I mean—until they came over a rise and found other grungy fairies at play. It looked like some kind of game of tag, but the people being chased kept diving into the mud and rolling around, and the chasers then had to leapfrog over them and chase someone else. Everyone was covered in muck and matted grasses.

Actually, no: it didn't look like a game of tag at all. It looked more like they were training for something. They were quiet and deadly serious.

Roland coughed loudly, as if he was about to make

an announcement, and soon the activity ended. The fairies—there were maybe a dozen of them—looked over at the group.

"Oh," said one of the smaller fairies, who was either bald or had close-cropped hair; there was so much mud, it was impossible to tell. *"Humans."*

Jojo could see, now that they were standing still, that the fairies were all injured in various ways. Under all that mud were bandages and bruises, and even a couple of crutches and slings. The short-haired (or bald) fairy that had just spoken had scratch marks running down its face and a bandage wrapped around its arm.

"This here," said Roland to the humans, "is fen fairyland. What's left of it."

The throne sat on the edge of the fen under a stand of birch trees that signaled the start of the forest. Around the throne—which was made of twigs and bark, just as the twins' replica throne had been—were the fairy throw-up and the mulberry juice, which they all now realized was actual fairy blood, not just pretend blood. The whole area smelled a little rotten. It was so much worse when it was the real thing and not a historical re-creation.

"Well, I've brung them like I promised," said Roland

to the other fairies, all of whom followed them to the throne area. He sat down, not on the throne, but near it on a hummock of grass that squelched and oozed under his weight. He slid his bare feet into a nearby puddle to soak and sighed with contentment as the chalky water swirled around his ankles.

The bald or possibly short-haired fairy started to speak. "What we need to do—"

"Wait, what is your name?" Jojo asked.

(I made Jojo ask that, dear reader, because I am tired of typing "bald or possibly short-haired fairy." But I am not making her do other things, just to be clear. She is doing all this stuff on her own. If I were actually in charge of this story, I would have told her to stay home and read a book on the front porch all afternoon, quiet and safe, and not venture into fairy-land at all. But alas.)

"What is your name?" Jojo asked.

"Peppercorn," said the fairy.

"Are you *he* or *she*?" asked Amy.

"Or another word?" said Bee. "Our cousin is *they*."

"Yes," said Peppercorn. "That sounds right. Now can we continue?"

Amy looked like she had more to say, but Theo said quickly, "Yes, and sorry for the interruption."

Peppercorn cleared their throat. "I'm the captain

of the fen fairies. We take turns, and this week is my turn. As leader, I've got something to say: we need your aid, humans. You know why. You know the prophecy because one of you wrote it." Peppercorn looked accusingly at the whole group, and Jojo cringed a little. Then Peppercorn cleared their throat. "Yes, good idea, share out the food."

And Jojo saw that another of the fairies had opened the cooler, which Theo had set down, and was ripping sandwiches into pieces and distributing them. Everyone, humans included, got a small, grimy corner of a sandwich before the food was gone. Then the fairies knelt by the puddles and drank the mucky whitish water, and they ate some of the grasses and flowers, too, and finished it all off with a blob of mud that looked like chocolate.

Jojo dipped her finger in the mud and licked, just in case. It did not taste like chocolate. Not at all.

"Please, help yourselves," said Peppercorn.

Maisie said faintly, "Thank you, but we're having a big dinner later, so we really shouldn't eat now." She gave her muddy sandwich corner to one of the fairies. Jojo had already eaten hers, dirt and all, as had the others.

Peppercorn spoke, mouth full of grass. "As you know, we need one of you to step up as queen—"

"Or king," added Roland, "if that's your thing."

"As ruler, and get rid of the bone creatures. Those monsters are coming back soon to attack us. We're helpless against them."

"Sitting ducks for sure," agreed Theo. "There's nowhere to hide."

Peppercorn shook their head, and mud flew off in spatters. "No, not ducks. The bone creatures are much smaller than ducks. And they're flying, not—"

"I didn't mean—" said Theo.

"And ducks aren't violent, at least not toward fairies. We think these bone creatures were possibly robins in their previous life."

"Robins have the hearts of killers, deep inside," said Roland. "They *look* cheerful, all red-chested and hopping around on people's lawns, but they're forever plotting murder."

"Murder of crows," murmured Theo.

"No, *robins*," said Peppercorn, in a tone that indicated they didn't think Theo was all that bright. "Anyway. We need a new queen to stop the bone creatures. The monsters will be back in two days—so that's how much time you have to decide which one of you will volunteer to stay here forever and be our ruler."

"Only two days?" said Jojo.

"That's *your* fault," said Roland in a *How could*

you forget? tone, and all the other fairies shifted, as if they were thinking, *Aha, SHE'S the one who made up the bone creatures!* "Remember your story about the bone birds?"

Numberless bone creatures flapped across the sky, their skeletal wings creaking, as they scouted for a fairy village to attack and pillage, which they did each week.... Yes, how could she forget?

Amy and Bee nodded emphatically. "'Each week,'" said Bee.

"The bone creatures first attacked us five days ago," said Peppercorn.

"Oooooh," said Bee, turning to Jojo. "Five plus two is seven. Seven is a week. That means in two more days . . ." She clapped her hands over her mouth in horror.

"In two days they'll be back," said Jojo.

"Hungry," said Peppercorn.

12

Home Again, Home Again, Jiggety-Jig

The five kids and Roland started walking back to the oak tree and its doorway to their own world. The bone creature was no longer circling in the sky, which was good, because if it had been, they would have had to walk *toward* it. But even though they couldn't see it, they knew it was out there somewhere, probably with its friends. Lurking.

As they stepped off the path to climb through the long grasses back to the oak tree, Maisie said, "Remember the noise we heard when we got here? Like a door opening and shutting again?"

Theo and Bee and Amy didn't remember, of

course, because they hadn't been paying attention, but Roland and Jojo remembered, and as they climbed the hill to the tree, they argued about what it could have been. Maisie was hoping that it was, as she put it, "just our imaginations playing tricks on us."

But it wasn't their imaginations playing tricks. Sitting next to the door, which on the fairyland side was bright red, was Fabio the cat, licking his paws and studying the travel party suspiciously, as if they might be treats. This was especially concerning because he was his usual size—which is to say, he towered over them like a giant.

"IT'S US, FABIO!" said Jojo in her biggest and most powerful voice. She didn't want to be a cat treat. "HOW DID YOU GET OUT OF THE HOUSE? BAD CAT!"

"Yes, bad kitty," crooned Bee, ruining all Jojo's sternness by speaking in a voice that suggested Fabio wasn't bad at all but very, very good. She ran up to him and wrapped her arms around his leg, though Maisie tried to pull her back.

"I don't ken how he got in here," said Roland. "The magic was only supposed to work for the people who built the fairy gardens. That was the five of you."

"I didn't build any fairy garden. I only looked at them," said Theo.

"You added a twig to mine," said Jojo. "Remember?"

"And Fabio helped with the historical replica," said Amy. "He rolled in it and we had to build around him, and he also tried to eat the dead bone creature."

"That's right," said Bee, reaching up to scratch under Fabio's enormous chin. She was barely as tall as his leg. "I had to promise him a snack to make him stop."

"So I got through the fairy door because I helped out a little—and Fabio got in for destroying things?" said Theo.

"That's how cats help," Maisie said gently. "It's not their fault."

Roland said, "But our magic was meant only to let in *persons*, and he's not a person. The cat, I mean."

"He is so!" said Bee. "Fabio's a person just as much as we are, and he's part of our family."

"Huh," said Roland, staring at the cat. Fabio stared back, blinking only after Roland did, like he was winning a staring contest. Then the cat yawned and stood up and scratched at the red door.

"All right," said Jojo, "we're going home."

"When you trot back here tomorrow," said Roland, "make sure you're all together, and lope through in the same order as how you did last time. That way the door will know you and let you in."

After they promised Roland they'd return the

next day and go through the door in the right order, they headed home.

Back in the human world, it was only midafternoon, not even close to suppertime, and the kids were all starving. They'd given away two entire lunches and had only a muddy sandwich bite each (and none at all for Maisie).

Maisie said she couldn't make more sandwiches. "We don't have enough bread left, and anyway," she added in a whisper to Jojo, "Mom would notice."

"You can come to my house and have cheese and crackers," said Theo. "I mean, my uncle's house."

"Are you sure your uncle won't mind?" asked Maisie. She looked like she wanted cheese and crackers very much.

Jojo, weak with hunger, said, "I'm sure it's fine, right, Theo?" and Theo grinned and nodded.

Maisie was too hungry to argue, so they agreed to go to Theo's, but Maisie insisted that they clean up first. Somehow they were covered in mud—almost as bad as the fairies. They even had muddy hair. "It must be because we were so small and close to the ground," Bee said. "The mud had more chance to jump all over us."

Theo ran home to wash up, and Maisie looked over

her sisters critically. "This is enough of an emergency that we should sneak in and shower." So they tiptoed in the back door, trying not to disturb their mom's work. Mom, fortunately, was talking on the phone with her editor, so there was no way she'd notice something as insignificant as the water running. Her words wafted faintly through the walls, from the upstairs office to the downstairs kitchen, where the girls deposited their muddy sandals and shoes on two paper towels Maisie placed on the floor.

Mom's voice was faint, but they could make it out. "So if Willow and Vlad have the argument about the cupcake shop *before* they kiss . . . ?" Silence as she listened to her editor's answer.

"Cupcakes are better than kissing," muttered Jojo.

Amy and Bee snort-giggled.

None of them wanted to read Mom's books. Too much romancy stuff.

(To be honest, Maisie wanted to read the books—someday, when she was older.)

Anyway: the bathroom and its shower were, fortunately for the sisters, just off the kitchen and not upstairs. So Jojo, who was muddiest, got in the shower first, while Bee and Amy tried to stand still and not touch anything in the kitchen, and Maisie tiptoed upstairs to fetch them all clean clothes. There were three bedrooms upstairs. One was Mom's, the second was Mom's office, and the third—the largest and sunniest and most gloriful bedroom—belonged to the four girls. It had a thick, soft ugly rug and a clackety radiator and giant windows and bright yellow walls, and it was the best place in the world to play on a rainy or gloomy day, except when Mom was on deadline and needed quiet.

In the bathroom outside the kitchen, Jojo stripped off her clothes and shoved them out the door just as Maisie had said to, got in the shower and even used soap, rinsed off, dried off, and stepped out of the bathroom wrapped in her towel.

"Your face is still muddy," said Amy. So Jojo hopped back in the bathroom and turned on the sink and scrubbed with a washcloth until her face was clean.

While Amy and Bee were showering, Jojo got dressed in the kitchen. Maisie took off her clothes and put on her bathrobe, which she'd also brought downstairs, and added her muddy shorts and T-shirt to the pile. Since everyone's clothes were now gathered, Jojo picked them all up and took them downstairs. She dumped them in the washer, added a scoop of detergent, and turned it on. Her job around the house was usually laundry, because she was good with big machines. Maisie, who was the most careful with knives, always made the sandwiches. The littles made beds. But none of the sisters cared if their beds were made, so mostly the littles did not make beds.

Maisie was the last to shower, and when she was done, they wiped up all the stray mud with their towels—the bathroom and kitchen floors were pretty bad—and Jojo brought the towels down to go in the next load of laundry.

Then, finally, they trooped over to Theo's house. Even though he was only one person instead of four, he was still in the shower. Theo's uncle let them in and said how pleased he was to meet them, just like they were grown-ups, and he told them they could call him Uncle Marcus like Theo did. He took them to the kitchen, where they sat at a battered wooden table and ate oranges. Theo's uncle was quite a bit older than their mom, they all thought, but he seemed nice. He was tall and thin, with a graying beard and glasses.

When Theo was done with his shower, they had cheese and crackers, and Theo's uncle asked them how their day was going and what they'd been up to in the woods. "Tell me everything," he said.

They glanced at one another. *Everything?*

13

Uncle Marcus's House

Needless to say, Maisie, Jojo, Bee, Amy, and Theo did not tell Uncle Marcus everything.

They didn't tell him that they'd met fairies who were muddy and liked to belch. They didn't tell him about the bone creatures or about the fairy queen's cruel, cruel death. They definitely didn't tell him they had only two days to make a decision about who would stay in fairyland forever and fight off the bone creatures and save the fen fairies. And they didn't say a word about how they'd been promised a magical reward and might, for example, turn into squirrels for an afternoon.

But no, thought Jojo. Not squirrels. They had to ask for something more important than that. Something that would fix everything that had gone wrong for their family in the last year. But what? She had no idea.

Anyway, there was a lot they didn't tell Uncle Marcus.

They *did* tell him about how fairyland could be found by walking through the blue door in the woods. They told him how small you had to shrink to fit through the door, and how everything, from flowers to mice, looked different when you were small. They told him what it was like to be so tiny in such a big, overwhelming world.

The thing was, Uncle Marcus thought they were making up a story. He listened carefully, slowly peeling and eating an orange as he pondered their words. And he asked good questions about how they all shrank to get through the door even though it *felt* like the door was growing and they were staying the same size, and he laughed at Amy's funny reenactment of wading through grass, and he shivered at Bee's description of the praying mantis. But he thought they were pretending; they could tell. He thought they were imaginative kids who had made up a story.

And in a way, Jojo thought, they *had* made it up. Hadn't they? I mean, didn't it all happen because of stories they'd told and gardens they'd built? Wasn't that what Roland had said?

But fairyland was also *real*, and that was confusing.

And it was waiting for them to make a decision.

When they'd finished the cheese and crackers and oranges, Uncle Marcus went back to reading his book in the living room, and the girls and Theo went back outside. This time they sat on Theo's front porch— which was really just a set of stairs leading up to the front door—instead of their own big porch.

Across the street, Fabio the cat sat on the big old stump and groomed himself at them. Every lick seemed accusatory. He was not going to forget they'd locked him in the house.

"Fabio didn't have to shrink at all to get through the blue door," said Bee, yawning. "He just poured himself through. Like milk."

Amy leaned on her twin's shoulder.

"We only have two days," said Theo. It was an entirely unnecessary thing to say.

"We *know*," said Jojo.

"The poor fairies," Maisie said. "But I don't see how we can help them. We can't stay in fairyland, not even just overnight. It wouldn't be safe. Anyway,

Mom would notice." Then she jumped a little and added quickly, "I mean, if we *had* a mom. I mean, the *librarian* would definitely notice."

Theo's uncle poked his head out the door. "Theo, I hate to break this up, but your dad said to remind you to practice violin. Best get that done now, before dinner."

Theo groaned.

Maisie looked at Uncle Marcus's watch and said, "Oh, it's late! We need to get home!"

Before they ran across the street, Theo said, "Come back after dinner? For a sleepover? And we can talk about . . . our made-up land."

What he really meant was, *We can talk about what to do in two days.* Jojo understood him immediately, and her sisters did too.

Uncle Marcus smiled. "That's a great idea—I'll walk over and ask your mom in a bit. We haven't really had a chance to do anything beyond wave at each other as we're coming and going, and it'll be good to meet my only neighbor."

Jojo bit her lip, not sure how to respond, since Theo thought they were all orphans.

Theo understood, though. He said to Jojo, "So . . . will your *mom* be home tonight?" He emphasized the word *mom* just a little bit, then leaned and whispered in Jojo's ear, "You know? The librarian? Will she be around to pretend?"

"Oh!" said Jojo. "Of course!" Then to Uncle Marcus she said, "Yes, our *mom* will be home tonight. Please do come over later."

"I'm sure it will be fine for us to do a sleepover," said Maisie. "I'm the oldest, and I'm in charge. I make sure everyone is safe all the time."

Uncle Marcus gave her a long, curious look. "Nevertheless," he said. "I need to make sure, too, and I need to introduce myself and tell your mom that you'll all be in sleeping bags together in the living room."

"We don't have sleeping bags," said Bee.

"Can we do blankets instead?" asked Amy.

"Of course," said Uncle Marcus. "Blankets will be perfect."

Jojo and her sisters ran in the back door just in time to help with dinner: the third and—they hoped—final night of burnt hotdish. This time there was also a big can of peaches to share. None of them were very hungry because of the oranges and the cheese and crackers, but they all took hotdish servings and pushed the food around on their plates so that it would not still be around for supper tomorrow.

At the end of dinner, as Mom was staring off into

space again, there was a knock at the front door.

"That's Uncle Marcus!" said Amy.

"Who?" said Mom. She stopped daydreaming.

Bee said, "He doesn't know about the front door being locked."

Jojo jumped up, ran out the back door and around the house, and brought Uncle Marcus to the back door. Mom seemed to know who he was by then.

After the two grown-ups talked, Mom said a sleepover was fine, but only after dishes were washed and showers taken. But they'd already taken showers, so getting ready was fast. Mom stayed out in the kitchen, helping with dishes, while they all found enough blankets and pillows. They didn't change into pajamas because they mostly just slept in shorts and T-shirts in the summer. It saved time getting dressed in the morning.

Finally, they needed only to brush their teeth. All four girls crowded into the bathroom, and Maisie held the tube and smooshed toothpaste on each brush so they could be quick.

Wiping her hands on a dish towel, Mom said, "Tomorrow is deadline." And suddenly everyone froze. Mom never missed deadline.

"Are you almost done?" asked Maisie.

"Very close," said Mom, smiling. "I think I'll make it."

Bee and Amy cheered and spit toothpaste. One of them—I think it was Bee—even managed to spit into the sink.

Mom said, "Tomorrow night, if I'm done, we should do something special for supper. I know things aren't like they were, when Grandma . . ." She took a breath and spoke again. "But I think we should plan something special for the end of deadline. Like we used to. Maybe pancakes. And then a game? Or a walk in the woods?"

Amy and Bee cheered.

Maisie nodded slowly, a careful smile on her face.

Jojo blinked. Pancakes and games and walks all sounded wonderful, like the old days. It used to be that when Mom was done with a writing project, Grandma made cookies, and they had a party and games, and it was like the whole world twirled around just for them. But without Grandma, could they celebrate? Should they even try?

Mom sighed. "I can't wait until tomorrow. I'm always so glad when deadlines are over."

And then Jojo remembered: They had their own deadline. *Two days.*

She glanced at Maisie, and she could tell Maisie was thinking the same thing. Two days to figure out who would stay in fairyland as queen. Two days to figure out how to defeat the bone creatures.

And, Jojo thought, two days to figure out what magic to ask for that would make them all happy again.

Jojo's stomach curled up in a little ball, like a big cat trying to sleep in a too-small box, but much, much less cozy. Worry and hope all smooshed together.

14

The Story of Grandma Nan's Cookies

The sleepover wasn't as much planning and decision-making as it was just *sleeping*—at least for most of the people there. At 9:00 p.m., after Uncle Marcus said to get in sleeping bags and blankets and turn out lights, the two youngest girls fell asleep almost as soon as their heads hit their pillows. Maisie stayed awake a few minutes longer, wondering aloud if they should leave the littles behind tomorrow, because they'd be safer away from the bone birds. ("Leave them with who?" said Jojo, and Maisie stopped wondering aloud.) She fell asleep soon after, even with her fears about her younger sisters; as Jojo explained to Theo, Maisie used to be a lot more fun, but not this past year. Theo explained back that Maisie had carried the lunch cooler the farthest of anyone, so maybe she was tired.

Theo, who was lying on his stomach, propped himself up on his elbows. He was wearing shorts and a T-shirt too, like the girls, but the bottom half of his body was hidden in a sleeping bag. "Tell me your stories about fairyland," he said. "Tell me the stories that . . . made all this happen."

Jojo, lying on her back and wrapped in her blanket like a burrito, wriggled her arms out and slapped them down at her sides. "It's not my fault."

"Oh," said Theo, "that's not what I meant. I just think the stories might help us come up with a solution. Maybe there's a clue in them."

Jojo rolled over on her stomach and made herself a mirror of Theo: propped on elbows, face in hands. Their heads were close for quiet talking. "The thing is," she said, "I told a *lot* of stories. Last year, that is. Not this year. I don't even remember all the stories I told. And some of them don't fit together."

"Why not this year?" asked Theo.

"What?"

"Why did you tell fairy stories last year but not this year?"

Jojo turned over and stared up at the ceiling. "Because last year we lived in town, and we . . . well, everything was different last year."

Theo said softly, "It was for me, too."

Jojo waited a minute for him to say how last year was different for him, but he didn't. And then she thought about how she hadn't known him very long—only a little more than two days!—but she already felt like he was a good listener. She could tell him what had happened. "Our grandma Nan got sick last summer," she said. "And then she was gone."

Theo didn't ask her to explain what "gone" meant. He already knew. "I'm really sorry," he said.

Across the room, Bee shifted in her blankets, and Amy muttered something in her sleep. Maisie snored, but in a delicate way.

"What was your grandma Nan like?" asked Theo. "I bet you miss her a ton."

Jojo shook her head. She wasn't sure she could say more. Not without crying.

"If you want to tell me?" said Theo.

She glared at the ceiling, thinking. Maybe telling about Grandma Nan in the dark, where no one could see her face, would be okay. "She took care of us a lot. And she lived next door, and we had a key to her apartment that we could use anytime we wanted to."

She could almost feel the key in her hand, the jagged edges rubbing her fingers. Talking about Grandma Nan didn't feel as bad as Jojo had thought it would. "She took us to the playground and the museum, and she picked Maisie and me up after school when we were little and walked us home, and she made amazing cookies. . . ."

"What kind?"

"What?"

"What kind of cookies?"

"Chocolate chip. The best kind. No nuts." Jojo rolled back onto her stomach and elbows to talk better. Theo nodded at her as if to say that he thought chocolate chip was the best too. "One time," she said, "long, long ago, when the twins were babies, Grandma Nan made cookies, but she put in too much baking soda. Actually, I was helping her, and we *both* put in too much baking soda, together. And the cookies turned out so bitter that we couldn't eat them. But when I was taking them out to the compost, I tripped, and they scattered all over the yard behind the apartment building, and even though we picked them up and composted them, there were still lots of crumbs on the ground. Grandma Nan said we were leaving food for the fairies." It was a good memory.

"And were the crumbs gone the next day? Did the fairies get them?"

"Maisie and Grandma and I watched out our window, and the squirrels and birds got them." Jojo had almost forgotten this part, but now it all came back to her: Grandma standing in the doorway of the bedroom while Jojo and Maisie knelt at the window and spied on the animals as they feasted on the lawn. "Maisie said, 'Those aren't fairies!' And Grandma Nan said that fairies sometimes come to us disguised as squirrels or birds."

"Your grandma sounds like she was fun."

Jojo nodded. This time when she needed to blink furiously, she didn't roll onto her back. She just let her eyes get wet and didn't worry that Theo might see.

Theo didn't seem to notice. "And she liked fairy stories. *Your* stories."

Jojo thought about the fairies that *hadn't* come when she asked them for magic. When Grandma Nan got sick. She thought about how nothing magical at all had jumped in to help. And suddenly she didn't feel sad anymore; instead, she felt hot and itchy. A little bit like she wanted to hit something. "Yeah," she said, "but after—later—I decided that fairy stories were silly. So I stopped telling them."

"And now it turns out they're real."

She nodded. It was strange. "The stories I told—
we told—came true. I thought they were just *stories*.
You know, like lies."

"I think lies are something different," said Theo.
"Stories are . . ." He waved his hand in a circle. "But
lies are trying to make someone believe something
you know isn't true."

Jojo nodded.

Theo sighed. "I need to tell you something."

"You do?"

"It's about—it's about my mom." His voice got
quiet, and Jojo scooched forward to hear him. "I kind
of lied to you. I acted like she's just away for the summer. But that's not true. She's—she's gone."

"Gone? Like—"

"Not dead," said Theo quickly. "I don't mean that.
Just *gone*."

Jojo wasn't sure what Theo meant. Of course she
was gone. "To Greenland." Greenland was a long way
away.

"No." His voice was so small, she could barely
hear him, even lying as still as she could. "I mean,
yes, she's in Greenland for the summer. But after the
summer she's not coming back to my house. My and
my dad's house. They're getting a divorce, and she
says I should live with my dad because he's home a

lot more. And dad says that too, but for the summer I came here because he's really busy at work right now." He took a deep breath and talked kind of fast, like he had to say it quick before he lost his courage: "I'm sorry I lied to you. I made you think my mom was just gone for the summer and everything was okay. But actually she doesn't want me."

And then he was completely silent. He lay down, face away from Jojo.

"Oh," said Jojo. She wanted to say, *I'm sure your mom wants you*, but she had never even met Theo's mom; how could she say that truthfully? *Most* moms wanted their kids, but maybe Theo's didn't. "I'm sorry, Theo. I'm really sorry."

They both lay quietly for a few minutes, breathing.

"Thank you," he said. "I feel better telling you."

Jojo thought. Theo's life wasn't good right now either. Kind of like theirs. He was missing someone too. Maybe the fairies could do something for him *and* for her and her sisters—something to make them not miss the people they were missing. Maybe something like that could be their magical gift.

But first, Jojo and Theo and Jojo's sisters had a job to do. "We need a plan," she said, "to help the fairies."

Theo wiped his hand across his face and half sat up, resting his chin in his hands again. "So, what stories did you tell about the fairies? Maybe if you can remember, then we can figure out how to help them."

"I never said anything about *fens*. I didn't even know what a fen was until today." What stories *had* she told? "But I did make up a story once about green fairies that were muddy and farted a lot, and the boy fairies had green beards. Maisie didn't like that one, so I only told it once. It was a long time ago."

"And the bone creatures?"

"They were the beginning of a story last summer, just before . . ." She wasn't going to tell about that day. "Right after we found a bird skeleton. I started a story about how the bone creatures attacked the fairy village every week. But—but I never finished it. And the idea that fairyland was ruled by a queen— that was a whole different story. I told that one last year, back when school was still going. It was after we read Narnia together with my mom."

"You mean the librarian."

"Yes, that." She wished now that she hadn't told that story about not having a mom. Maybe she should confess to Theo that the librarian was pretend.

But Theo's mind was in fairyland. "In the story

about the bird skeleton . . . how many bone creatures were there? And how did the people in the story defeat them?"

This was the miserablest part. Jojo said, "The bone creatures were infinite. That's what I said. I said 'numberless.' And no one defeated them; I never actually finished the story. And then later Amy and I got in an argument about if things could really *be* numberless. I said they could, in fairyland. And she said that even ants could be counted, it would just take a really long time to count them, and no creature was numberless. And I got mad at her and . . . then lots of things happened." Grandma Nan. The hospital. The small funeral. "And we never got back to the story."

Theo was quiet for a really long time. Jojo thought he might be drifting off to sleep, even though he was half sitting, and she wondered if his head would slide gradually down to the pillow when he fell all the way asleep, or if it would thunk. She was thinking, *It will thunk*, when Theo spoke again.

"I wonder . . . if we can make up a new story. Or if we can think about the old stories in a new way. 'Numberless,' but what does that mean? 'Undefeated,' but only because you didn't finish the story. We . . . need a plan that . . . uses these ideas. . . ."

His head slid gracefully down to the pillow. And he was asleep.

Jojo, the last to travel to dreamland, was also the last to wake up the next morning, but not by much, because everyone else was making so much noise. Uncle Marcus cooked pancakes and scrambled eggs, and when he heard that everyone was planning to trek to the fairy door, he made them sandwiches and told the girls to go home and check with their mom before running through the woods. Maisie carried the blankets and pillows home and came back with the cooler to pack the food in, and also told Uncle Marcus she'd checked with Mom.

Jojo looked at Maisie with a special look. Maisie looked back at Jojo and then said in Jojo's ear, "I did, really. She's not writing. She's cleaning the house."

Cleaning the house meant that Mom was done with her deadline and back in the world.

Jojo and Maisie went outside and sat on the steps while they waited for the others to finish eating. "I don't think she slept last night," said Maisie. "She said she emailed the manuscript to her editor early this morning."

Well. That was good news for Mom, but not-so-great news for fairyland. Jojo and her sisters and Theo would have to figure out the fairyland problem today, because by tonight Mom would be done cleaning and sleeping and would want to do fun things with her daughters.

"We should leave the littles with her today," said Maisie. "I don't think it's safe for them to go back to fairyland. They're so small, a bird could pick them up and eat them."

"Mom needs to sleep," said Jojo. "If she was up all night writing."

"Still . . . ," said Maisie.

"I'll help watch them today, and so will Theo. Anyway, Amy and Bee won't stay behind. You know they won't—they'll follow us, and that would be way more dangerous than us bringing them."

Maisie scrunched her nose, thinking. "That's probably true. I'll be able to take care of them better if they're with us. It's safer that way."

Jojo rolled her eyes, not even caring if her older sister saw. Maisie never used to be such a worrywart. She had always been more careful than Jojo, but she had been *fun*. And now she was just . . . "Anyway," said Jojo, "stop trying to be the mom. You're not her."

Maisie frowned. "At least I'm trying—"

"Trying what?" said Amy.

"I tried syrup on my eggs," said Bee. "And it was good."

Everyone was suddenly on the front steps, Theo holding the cooler of sandwiches. "We should go," he said. "We have a mission to complete. After we figure out exactly what it is."

15

Fabio Refuses

This is not going to work," said Amy, about an hour into the morning. The kids had located the cat, after searching all his favorite spots in their yard, under the lilacs. Jojo had then lured Fabio into a lidded basket with treats inside, but Fabio ate all the treats immediately and was now trying to escape—and Amy, who had once been shut into a closet by mistake when she was a toddler, was on his side. "Set him free. Fabio doesn't like being trapped in there."

That was true. Fabio was mewling pitifully inside the basket, and all they had done so far was cross the street toward Theo's house and the woods.

"I know," said Jojo. "But he should be going to fairyland with us—and you know he won't if I let him out." She didn't open the lid yet; she was still hoping he'd decide to love the basket.

"We can lure him to fairyland with more treats," said Bee. "He'll come if we leave a trail of food. Like Hansel and Gretel's bread crumbs, but backward."

"Sideways," said Theo.

"I guess that might work," said Maisie doubtfully. "But he just ate breakfast, and he doesn't always want more, you know."

"I don't know why not," said Bee.

"I do," said Jojo. "Sometimes getting in trouble is more fun than treats."

Theo rubbed a scratch on his arm. It wasn't from Fabio, but it *was* from crawling through scratchy bushes to find Fabio. "Maybe we should just let him go, and if he decides to come into fairyland, then he decides to. It doesn't seem like a good idea to force him. Like, maybe that's a bad omen."

"Fine," said Jojo, grumpy mostly because it had been her idea to find Fabio. Roland had said that they should all return today—and in the same order they entered fairyland before. By Jojo's reasoning, that meant that Maisie, the last person to go through the door, should take Fabio with her, holding his basket just behind her back so he would be entering last. If they were really going to follow the rules, then Fabio should come too.

But Fabio was definitely not interested in riding through the blue door in a basket. Jojo opened the lid, and the cat leapt out and then shambled a few feet away, where he flopped down, stretched out like a crescent moon, and glared at them. Slowly his eyes closed, but the tip of his tail twitched continuously.

Amy said, "Why do we need to bring Fabio with us, anyway? We didn't last time. So it would be following the rules *not* to bring him again."

Jojo thought about the issue as they walked through the woods toward the little blue door, and she had to admit (though to herself only) that Amy had a good point. It was true: they hadn't taken Fabio along the first time; he'd gone through on his own. Either he'd do that again today or he wouldn't. You can't control cats.

I mean, who *can*?

The five kids went through the door just like last time, but without Roland in the lead: first Jojo, then Amy and Bee, then Theo, then Maisie with the food cooler. (Jojo had carried the cooler through the woods, because when Maisie said she was still tired from carrying it yesterday, Theo offered to carry it for a while; but that didn't seem fair to Jojo, since he'd lugged it a lot yesterday, so Jojo said she *wanted* to carry the cooler, since she wasn't holding the cat basket anymore. Anyway, the short version is: Maisie carried the cooler through the door, to make things as close to yesterday as possible.)

They all waded through the tall grass to the dirt road, then took the dirt road toward fen fairyland. Today, behind them—

Behind them flapped at least *three* bone creatures, low in the sky, circling and turning. It was hard to count exactly how many there were, because one or two would swoop down out of sight, and then one or two would fly up again, and no one could tell if the ones that flew back up were new creatures or just the same bone creatures over and over again. But—

"At least three," said Maisie from the lead, looking over her shoulder at the sky. Three were visible now, the most they'd seen at one time.

Theo and Jojo walked together at the back end of the line. "'Numberless,'" Theo murmured.

Grimly, Jojo nodded.

When the kids got to fen fairyland, no one was there.

No one.

Not a single fairy.

Just an empty fen.

What had happened to the fen fairies? They yelled for Roland and Peppercorn and the others, but no one came. They waited and waited, then they walked carefully all around the edges of the fen, peering into the woods, finally gathering near the throne under the birch trees.

"We might as well eat lunch," said Bee, dropping onto the damp ground.

Amy flopped down next to her, then jumped up. "I'm all wet!" After she turned and turned, trying to see her muddy backside, she shrugged and sat down again. "Oh well."

Jojo and Theo sat too. They'd dry off later. And if some members of the group were going to be muddy, they might as well all be muddy.

Maisie handed out the sandwiches and then sat on the cooler like it was a bench, her scratched-up legs (yes, from looking for Fabio) blocking part of the HUMAN ORGANS sticker, so that all it said was HUM—ANS.

And then, all of a sudden, Roland was standing in front of them, as if he'd appeared from nowhere, even muddier than yesterday, scratching his armpit and stretching. "I been meaning to query," he said, "if there really are humans in those sandwiches."

"Oh!" said Maisie. She fell off the cooler and landed with a squelch on the ground.

"Ah, just human organs. I see now."

"No," said Jojo. "It's an old cooler that a friend of . . . our librarian . . . gave us. She's a doctor. The friend is, I mean."

"There are *plant* organs in the sandwiches," said Bee. "Delicious plant hearts and livers and entrails." She took a big bite.

Maisie retrieved a sandwich from the cooler and handed it to the muddy fairy. (They'd asked Uncle Marcus to make two sandwiches for each of them, for just this reason.) And suddenly—from nowhere, it seemed—Peppercorn was there, and so were the rest of the fen fairies. All of them impossibly grimy.

The fairies devoured the sandwiches.

But they seemed really worried as they ate.

"So," said Peppercorn with a full mouth. "Have you decided? Which of you is going to sit on the throne? And can you climb up there right away, before the bone creatures come back?"

"But they aren't coming until tomorrow," said Theo. "Yesterday you said two days."

"No. Two days ago I said two days," said Peppercorn.

"What?" said Maisie.

Roland slapped his forehead. "Did I forget to mention? Time runs different here than in your world."

They all stared at him.

Jojo said, "That makes sense, though. Wasn't that true in Narnia, too? I based some of my fairyland stories on stuff in the Narnia books." But if time moved differently here, that meant they'd never know how many days would pass between visits, and next time they came back, it might be tomorrow, or it might be two days later, or a hundred years. . . .

"Wait, *today*?" yelped Maisie, her eyes big. "The bone creatures are coming back *today*?"

"Any minute," said Peppercorn, bouncing a little on their feet. "That's why we were all hiding. We worried you weren't coming. We dug tunnels." Peppercorn sounded a little accusatory.

"Tunnels seem like a great solution," said Theo.

The fen fairies all groaned. One smaller one splatted down on the ground like she couldn't go on.

"The thing is," said Roland, still standing ankle-deep in the puddle from which (they now understood) he'd emerged, "we love rolling around in the mud and all. It's great for the skin. So healthy like. But we don't want to *live* under the mud. That'd be like asking you humans to kip under a pile of broccoli. Wholesome, but not comfortable long term, right?"

"We need to see the sky," said the small fairy in a plaintive voice, looking upward. Then her voice changed. "Oh no . . ."

Without wanting to look, all of them—fairies and humans alike—glanced at the sky, toward where the bone creatures had been circling earlier that morning.

One skeletal creature near the horizon circled, then dove. The bone creatures were gone. The slate-gray sky was completely empty, except for a few smudges of almost-erased clouds. Where had the monsters gone?

Suddenly the fen fell silent. The crickets and the bees and the flies and the birds—all the things that normally spun a curtain of noise in the fen and kept it feeling alive and happy—disappeared. There was not even the shushing of the breeze rustling the sedge grasses.

They all stared up and away some more. The sky was blank and ominous.

16

Bone Creatures, Numberless

A nd then, from far off, everyone could hear flapping. It was an odd kind of flapping, not the sound that bird wings make in our world, but the sound that wings without flesh or feathers might make—sort of like twigs swooshing quickly through the air. But more creaky, like wicker.

In the distance they saw bone birds flying toward them.

"'Numberless,'" murmured Jojo.

Amy heard her. "'Numberless' isn't real." She looked up at the sky, trying to count. But the creatures were dipping and swirling too much.

"Does that mean . . . ," said Maisie.

"These bone birds are numberless," said Theo. "Infinite. Because that was the story."

Bee took Jojo's hand and patted it. "It's okay. You didn't mean to."

It was true, she didn't. She'd just been trying to tell a good story. But none of that mattered now. They had to help the fairies, somehow, even if the bone creatures never stopped coming. Even if they were numberless.

The fairies—

The five kids looked around. The fairies were gone. Bubbles rose from the mud around them.

Roland's head popped back up. "Dive!" he yelled. "Dive quick, and dig, and stay down for as long as you can hold your breath—at least three hours." He plunged back into the mud.

There was another silence then, broken only by the louder and louder flapping of broken-twig wings as the bone creatures grew closer.

"We . . . can't hold our breath . . . for three hours . . . can we?" asked Bee.

Amy shook her head.

"Not even for three minutes," said Theo.

"Quiet," said Jojo, holding up her hand. "We need a plan. Right now."

Maisie pulled out a lonely last half sandwich. "We can try to bribe them with food."

That seemed like a good plan.

(Actually, no one thought it was a good plan. But it was the only plan they had, so they tried to imagine it was a good one. And after all, the fairies had liked the sandwiches, so maybe the bone birds would too?)

They placed the sandwich on top of the cooler like an offering and stepped back from it, away from the approaching bone birds. Without discussing anything, they all took one another's hands and waited for the end.

Bone creatures don't eat sandwiches. You know this already, right?

Five of these not-birds, these flying skeletons, soared toward them. As they winged closer, the kids could hear their old-wicker-furniture bones creaking louder and louder. They flapped their wings slower than normal birds, but they seemed to fly faster. Their beaks jutted out of their skulls like knives. Other than the beaks, though, the creatures looked almost delicate, lacy. And so far there were only five of them.

But there were surely more on the way.

When the five bone creatures—only a little smaller than Maisie and definitely bigger than Amy and Bee—

landed on tufts of fen grass near the lunch cooler and peered their skeletal heads forward to examine the sad little sandwich, Bee giggled.

Bee snickered sometimes when she was scared. She wasn't trying to be rude. But the bone creatures didn't know that.

"Are you laughing at us, human child?" croaked the one nearest to the sandwich, tilting its skull to the side and clacking its knife-sharp beak. "And are you offering us sandwiches to torment us?"

"Um . . . no?" whispered Bee, hiccupping.

A smaller bone bird in the back creaked, "You must know we can't eat sammiches. Where would the bite go after we swallowed?"

"We were trying to be nice," said Maisie. She put her arm around Bee's shoulders and stood as tall as she could.

"Nice," scoffed a third bone creature. It said the word with a lingering *s*, like *"Nicccccccccce,"* hissing toward them and ending with its beak wide open, so they saw down its mouth all the way to where the base of the skull attached to the spine. Jojo wondered if her own bones worked the same way. She touched her neck carefully.

"Does that mean you don't eat fairies, either?" asked Bee, her voice cracking.

"We definitely eat fairies," said the biggest bone creature. "The pity is that we can't swallow them properly."

There was a short, appalled silence.

"There are only five of you," said Amy, stepping mostly in front of Bee and putting her hands on her hips. "That's not numberless."

The biggest bone creature cackled. "It is if you don't know numbers. What is five, anyway? We don't even know what *five* means. We are *numberless*. We have no numbers."

"Onetwothreefourfive," said Amy.

All the bone creatures shook their heads slowly, grinning their beaky, bony grins. Jojo could see their vertebrae rotating like gears.

"We don't know what that word means," said the smallest bone creature. "Are you even speaking English?"

Amy shook her head in disgust and stepped back, glowering. Maisie pulled her in and held both twins close, and Theo stared at the creatures like he was in a trance.

It was up to Jojo now.

The skeletons scratched at the mud with their bony bird feet. All five of them glared at the kids, and suddenly they flapped their wings like they were going to fly up in the air and attack.

"*What,*" said Jojo, desperate to stop them, "do you *want*? Maybe we can make a deal."

"A deal!" croaked a bird in the back. "HAHAHA-HAHAHA!"

And all the other bone birds cried, "HAHAHAHA-HAHA!" Their voices sounded almost like a wail, loud and unworldly.

"What do we *want*?" said the biggest bone crea-ture, the one nearest the sandwich. It seemed to be the leader of the group. "We *want* to attack the fairies. What kind of deal can you offer us for that? How about this: give us the fairies and we'll leave you alone. At least for today. HAHAHAHAHAHAHA!"

The other bone creatures joined in again: "HAHA-HAHAHAHAHA!"

Theo shook his head quickly, like he was waking up from a dream. "But why . . . do you want to attack the fairies? What did they ever do to you?"

"They did nothing," said the big bone bird, shrug-ging its skeletal wings. "We just want to. Is that so bad?"

"Well, yes!" said Maisie, her arms still around Bee and Amy. "It is. Bad."

The bone creatures all blinked. I don't know how they did that without eyeballs and eyelids, but I promise you that all five of the kids saw the monsters blink right at this moment. They blinked as if they had never before considered that they were bad. As if they were surprised.

And Jojo thought, for just a second or two, that maybe things would be okay.

But then the leader shrugged its bony shoulders. "Huh. Okay, then. I guess we're Bad. But that's *your* fault, you know. You made us this way. In your story."

"You can choose," Maisie said. "You don't have to be bad—"

The bone bird leader suddenly hopped forward, darted its head toward Bee, and snapped its beak. Bee screamed. Maisie yanked Bee and Amy back, dragging them away from the birds.

"It bit me!" cried Bee.

"Get away!" yelled Maisie at the flock.

The bone bird clicked its beak like scissors. "We're the best bad creatures *ever*."

And the others joined in: "EVERRRRRRRR!"

"We're the best! The baddest! If you won't give us the fairies, we'll eat youuuuuuuuu!"

"YOUUUUUUUUUU!"

And they all swarmed up into the air, creaking and flapping.

The Second Great Fairy War

Jojo and Theo rushed over to Maisie and the twins. Maisie was panting like she'd just run a race, and her eyes were huge. Bee was holding her arm against her stomach. "It's okay," she said. "I'm okay." She patted Maisie's face with her free hand. Amy gripped Bee's shoulder.

Jojo looked around wildly, but there wasn't anywhere to run to. That is the problem with a fen: there isn't much *there*. I mean, fens are beautiful in a stark, wet, minimal way, with every color meaning something and every plant brave and important. But they don't give you anywhere to hide.

So the sisters and Theo stood unprotected in the fen, while the bone birds swarmed up, swirling, converging into a point high above them, merging into a single dot. Then—

"We need to do something!" said Jojo. But what? She looked at Theo.

Theo said, "What happened in your story?"

"It never got this far," said Jojo. She'd never finished the bone bird story; didn't he remember?

Above them, the dot got bigger—

And split apart into five dots—

And the bone birds were diving, piercing down through the sky. One for each kid, stabbing toward them.

"Make up an ending *now*," said Theo. His eyes were so big, they took up his whole face. "Jojo! Make an ending!"

Of course. A new ending to fix things. But what? "Um . . ."

"*Hurry!*" said Theo.

Maisie threw her arms over the twins.

"After they flew up into the sky," said Jojo quickly, feeling completely lost, "at that moment, the bone birds forgot—they forgot that they could be broken. And they *could* be, because they were built like—like a magnet set. And then someone helped the kids—someone unexpected. . . ."

It was the worst story ending ever.

Maisie gasped, and Jojo looked up again. The birds were still diving straight down at them. Jojo threw her arms up to cover her head—

And then—

Then—

The gigantic cat Fabio, so slow in their own world—

But somehow so fast here—

Leapt above them and swatted the bone birds out of the sky. And the monsters fell apart, like busted magnet creations, pieces everywhere.

Fabio sat down on his haunches and licked his front paw. Around him, the bone creatures lay unmoving, broken into numberless pieces.

Jojo took a deep breath.

Beside her, Theo whispered, "It worked!"

Maisie burst into tears.

Amy said, "Ugh, you're squashing me," and struggled out of her older sister's grip.

"Fabio! Good kitty!" Bee struggled away from Maisie too, and both twins threw themselves on Fabio's enormous body to hug him, though he ignored them and kept grooming himself.

Theo sat down hard on the ground, as if suddenly he couldn't stand up anymore.

Maisie kept crying.

Jojo cleared her throat. There was a bit more to do. She had to finish the story. "And then the bone birds fell apart," she said, "like magnet toys when a cat swipes at them, and the kids rebuilt their broken pieces into . . . a fairy table, so that the fairies could . . . eat their sandwiches . . . at a table . . . if they wanted to."

It wasn't the best ending she'd ever made, but it was all she could think of at the moment. And it was important to finish the story and make sure the bone creatures stayed destroyed. "The bone birds never returned to fairyland ever again," she said. "The end."

For a few moments no one spoke. Maisie wiped her face and shuddered.

Then Theo said, "Well. I guess we better build a table." He picked up a vertebra and wandered off.

"Bee," said Maisie, hiccupping, "are you okay? Really okay?"

"I'm fine," said Bee, leaning against Fabio's side and inspecting her arm. She sounded disappointed. "I thought I might get a big scar like a pirate, but I'm hardly even bleeding. See?" She held up her arm, where there was a bruise already and a tiny dot of blood.

Maisie sucked in a breath. "You could have—something really bad could have happened."

Bee shrugged. "But it didn't."

Amy said, "Theo, I'll help you build the table." She started picking up bone pieces. Bee followed.

Maisie started crying *again*. She sat on the cooler and sobbed.

Jojo knew she needed to talk to Maisie. When your sister is upset for no good reason, it's your job to find out what's wrong.

But she didn't know what to say. So she sat on the cooler next to Maisie, which was so small for two people that they were both almost falling off the sides.

Maisie took a shuddery breath and swiped at her face with a muddy hand. "It was my fault," she said.

What? "No. The bone bird—"

"Last year. When Grandma died. It was my fault." Maisie scrubbed at her eyes. Her entire face was smeared with mud.

"What do you mean?" said Jojo.

"When she got sick, I should have gone to our apartment and gotten Mom right away. Instead of letting Grandma take a nap. I should have . . ." Maisie shook her head. "But I didn't know she was so sick." Her eyes welled up again, and her face fell apart. "I'm sorry." She crumpled against Jojo, and Jojo squished close so they wouldn't slip off the cooler.

"It's *not* your fault," she said. "I promise. And Bee is okay. And none of this is your fault either."

Maisie sniffed.

It also wasn't Jojo's fault. She knew that. Or the fairies' fault. Sometimes bad things just *happened* and no one knew why. Jojo put her arm around Maisie.

"Ask Mom sometime," said Jojo. "She never lies. Grandma was just—she was just really, really sick. All of a sudden." Jojo thought about that day, how awful it was: the quiet apartment after Mom took Grandma to the hospital, the flowers and food deliveries after Grandma didn't come back, the packing boxes and the move to the country, where they didn't live near any friends. But Jojo was starting to realize that there were also good parts to her memories. "Do you remember when we found the dead bird on the ground and she bent over to see it too? She let us stop and look even though she wanted to go home and take a nap. She knew we wanted to talk about the bird, and she even pointed out the nest."

"She was the best grandma ever," said Maisie.

Jojo squeezed Maisie's shoulder. The cooler was exactly the right size to hold them both—exactly as close together as they should be right now. Maisie leaned her head against her sister's.

"She was the best ever," agreed Jojo.

In the aftermath of the bone-bird-and-cat battle, Theo and Bee and Amy—and later, Jojo and Maisie— built a table for the fairies, with bird vertebrae for legs and, for the tabletop, wing bones covered with birch bark. The pointy beaks became scissors, in case the fairies ever wanted to cut their sandwiches instead of ripping.

"But they won't want to," said Amy. "They like to rip better."

Bee nodded. In the dappled sunlight, her bruise looked like a hero's tattoo.

While the kids built the table, Fabio draped himself over the too-small throne, which immediately collapsed beneath him, and sunned himself, one eye occasionally flicking open and glancing upward, as if to be sure there was nothing else he should knock out of the sky.

He's so slow at home, and so fast here, thought Jojo. *But that makes sense. It's like time. Cats are different here.*

As the kids finished building the table, the ground began to bubble, and soon the fairies stood on the surface of the fen, glopped with mud and delighted to learn the bone creatures were gone forever.

After hearing the story of how Fabio had saved them all, the fairies gathered around the cat to thank him. He was asleep, still curled on the flattened throne.

Theo wandered off to find the perfect flower to decorate the fairy table.

Peppercorn asked the girls, in a soft voice so as not to wake the feline hero, "Have you decided who will stay as ruler?"

The girls all looked at one another. Maisie shrugged apologetically. "Our mom just finished writing her book, and we're supposed to go home tonight and celebrate. . . . And Theo's uncle expects him home for dinner. . . ."

"But the prophecy," said Peppercorn.

There was a miserable silence.

Jojo stared at the cat curled on the throne. They—that is, the group of them, Fabio included—had saved the fairies, but the fairies wouldn't feel truly safe until the prophecy was fulfilled. And they wouldn't give the girls and Theo a magical gift until the prophecy was fulfilled either. Jojo wanted to kick herself for making up such a dopey prophecy. Why did fairyland have to be ruled by a human, anyway? The fairies would do a much better job ruling themselves. They already knew how they wanted to live.

The cat opened both eyes. He looked directly at Jojo and blinked. And blinked again. It was like a code.

"That's it!" said Jojo.

"What's it?" said Theo, carrying a daisy the size of his head.

"Do you remember the prophecy?" Jojo asked her sisters. "I mean do you remember the words *exactly*?"

Maisie shook her head. "Not word for word."

Jojo could finally see a solution. "Do *you* remember the exact words?" she said to the fairies.

Peppercorn nodded. "Of course. It's carved on a rock—somewhere back here." They dug behind Fabio and the now-flat throne and pulled out a small slab and read. "'One of the people who is about to go through the doorway from human land to fairyland will become the new ruler, and the new ruler will save the fairies.' Exact words."

"That's right," said Jojo. "One of our *people*—but not necessarily a human."

"Oh!" said Theo, a light dawning in his eyes.

"And who would be a better queen—"

"Ruler," said Theo.

"—than the one who knocked the bone birds out of the sky? He's even already sitting on the throne!" Jojo gestured grandly, and at that moment Fabio raised his head in a particularly regal pose. Then he hunched around and started licking the spot right under his tail, which was much less regal. "Fabio will be your king," said Jojo quickly. She could see that Peppercorn was about to say something, and she didn't want to give them a chance to argue, not yet. "Or queen, if you like that better. He doesn't care. Your ruler. Listen, he's the hero, not us, and he can protect you if anything like a bone creature ever comes back."

"How will we glue him down on the throne? Or the . . . throne area?" asked Roland. "As I recollect, you couldn't even get him to stay inside your house."

"That's the most perfect part of this plan," said Jojo, and Theo nodded beside her. "He doesn't *need* to stay. Don't you see? The prophecy doesn't say the ruler needs to stay in fairyland full-time. Just that they need to *become* ruler here. Fabio can be your royalty today, and then he can go home for a bit, and you can do fine on your own. He can get in and out of fairyland by himself, as he's proved twice now. So he'll come back to check on you."

"Will he?" said Peppercorn, furrowing their eyebrows.

"I'm sure he will," said Jojo.

"He *will*," said Maisie. "Look at him. He loves it here. This is the first time he's ever caught a bird, *ever*. He'll definitely be back. Especially if you tell him he's the queen."

Fabio was sitting on his haunches now, scanning the sky, his tail swishing. He looked impressive again, like a ruler guarding his land. It was a good look for convincing the fairies.

Peppercorn sighed. "Fine. Hail to our new queen."

Fabio nodded serenely to the fairies. Then he curled up again on the throne, and they gathered around and argued about who got to pet him first.

"I'll make a grooming schedule," said Peppercorn, "so that we can all take turns. Fair and square." They turned and saw the table. "What is . . . that?"

"I hope you don't mind," said Theo. "We built you a table."

"A *what*?" said Roland.

They explained what a table was for.

"But we could also just sit in the mud and eat out of our hands, right?" said Roland. "I mean, if we want to rough it, we can try the table, but for real nosh and civilized dining we'll still eat in the normal way, right?" He sounded a little anxious.

"It's okay," said Jojo. "The table pieces are like a

magnet set." Then she realized they might not know what that meant. "They come apart, and you can stick them back together in different ways and build whatever you want. You don't have to leave it in a table shape. You can change it."

"Oh," said Peppercorn in obvious relief. "Well, that's good—I mean, it was kind of you to build this tadel for us."

"Table," said Bee.

"Right. It was kind of you. We might make it into something else someday, when we forget what a table is for."

"Today," said Roland. "We'll probably forget later today."

Jojo smiled. Fairies who didn't want to remember tables seemed like a happy enough story ending to her.

And then she knew. She knew what the magical gift should be. And it was so good, she didn't even need to discuss it with the others. Because it would fix things for all of them.

"Roland," she said, "I need to talk to you."

The Magical Gift

Jojo's sisters were celebrating with the other fairies, laughing and stomping and splashing in the mud—even Maisie, who sometimes acted like she was too grown up for rolling around in muck. Jojo and Roland walked a short distance away so they could talk in quiet. Theo followed them.

Jojo said, "Don't you want to hang out with the others?"

Theo shook his head. "I'd rather be here when you ask for your favor. If that's okay."

"Fine," she said, frowning. "Just don't . . . interrupt or anything." She took a deep breath.

Roland's face twisted all of a sudden, and some dried mud flaked off where his forehead wrinkled. "I might gotta go join the others. . . ."

"After the favor," said Jojo.

The fairy dipped his head, grimacing. "I know what you're thinking on."

"You know? Because of fairy magic? Can you read my mind?"

"I know because I know *you*. You slapped me together, remember? I know you like a snail knows its own slime." Roland belched. Then he said, "I can't do it, you know."

She stared at him. "You can."

"Can't."

"Can't what?" said Theo.

Roland answered in a surprisingly gentle voice. "Can't take away her and her sisters' memories of their grandma." He jutted his chin at Theo. "Or your memories of your mom."

Theo's mouth dropped open.

"You *can*," said Jojo. "Just think about it for a minute. It's perfect. If we don't remember, then we don't feel sad. I'm not asking you to completely erase our brains. Just to take away . . . to take away . . ." She couldn't think of the word she wanted.

"The grief," said Roland. "And no. I can't do it. I am," he added, "truly sorry."

Grief. That was the word. Roland knew her thoughts. And because she'd made him up, Jojo knew Roland, too. He was like the inside of the deepest part of herself—but somehow he was also his own self. And he was wrong. He *could* do it. He just didn't want to try. She'd made up a whole world by telling stories—she and her sisters had—so surely a fairy with magic could erase a few painful memories with his own story or spell?

"Nope," said Roland. "I'm blasted sorry, kinchin. When some dishes get smashed, you can't glue them back together. Not even in fairyland."

Not even in fairyland. But it wasn't fair. Jojo's eyes were all of a sudden stinging, and Roland was turning blurry. "Grandma Nan—"

"—is one of those things. There's no magic that will make you stop missing her." He rubbed his nose, ducked his head, and slowly walked away.

Theo sat next to Jojo in the mud as she cried.

When it was time to go home, the four sisters and Theo left Fabio behind in fairyland, being scratched under his chin by three fairies at once; he'd return to their world when he got hungry. Carrying the empty cooler in turns, they walked back: down the dirt road, through the tall grass, out the red door (blue on the human side). Jojo and Theo and Roland—who said he'd accompany them as far as the back lawn of Theo's house—were the last to go through the door. Full-sized, Jojo's sisters ran ahead of them through the woods, calling and laughing.

Jojo and Theo and Roland neared the end of the forest. Jojo was determined not to cry again.

Theo cleared his throat. "Do you think we'll go back someday? To fairyland?"

Roland said, "That would be up to you. You have a magical wish owed you, after all."

"Yes!" said Theo. "I mean, we'll have to vote on it. But yes."

From far ahead, Bee called back to them. "Hurry up, Joey! Mom's probably ready to play now!"

"Come home with us and meet our mom, Theo!" yelled Amy.

Theo flicked a glance at Jojo.

Jojo sighed, suddenly very tired. "We . . . have a mom." She couldn't even remember anymore why she'd made up that weird story about not having a mom, and it felt like it hardly mattered, except . . . maybe Theo would be mad? He had a right to be, after all; she'd lied to him. And she hadn't even confessed after he told her about *his* mom. "I'm sorry. We're not orphans at all. Our mom was just really busy with work stuff. Deadline."

"I know," said Theo. "Not about the deadline, but about the rest. I knew all along you had a mom. I just thought it was a good story."

"Oh," said Jojo. "Good." Maybe she hadn't lied after all.

When Jojo and Theo and Roland reached the end of the woods, Theo stepped out onto the lawn behind his uncle's house. Roland said, "This is where I scarper, missy. We fairies don't like your short, fancy grasses."

Jojo paused at the edge of the woods. It felt like they were all leaving something important behind— and moving to something important ahead. Grandma Nan was gone, and missing her felt like a wound that would never heal.

Theo turned back to Jojo. "Are you coming?" Behind him lay his uncle's house, and beyond that, the road, and across the road, their own house and their wide porch. Mom was rocking on the porch with a big bowl on her lap.

Bee and Amy ran to her, yelling, "We went to fairyland!"

"Tell me all about it!" called Mom. "I made cookies!" She held up the bowl.

Maisie followed the twins across the lawn to the road.

Jojo had to ask Roland, one last time. She had to. Just in case. "Are you sure you really can't . . . ?"

The fairy didn't answer for a moment, and when he lifted his face to her, Jojo saw that tears had cleaned the mud away from his cheeks in stripes. He shook his head.

And Jojo thought, *I'll never feel better. I'll always have a giant bruise on my heart. I'll always miss her.* For a second, the world froze. Maybe this was how her life would be from now on: lots of little frozen moments where she hurt too much to move.

And then the world slowly thawed and started moving again, and Roland was still there, standing next to her with his streaky face and gazing out at Uncle Marcus's yard. And Theo stood on the other side of her. He took her hand.

"I've been thinking about something," Theo said. His hand was warm and squeezed hers steadily. "You tell great stories, Jojo. I know it's not the same as having your grandma back. But—I really liked the story you told me last night. I never even met her, and you showed me what a great lady she was and how much she loved you. Remember the bitter cookies?"

"Oh, the bitter cookies," laughed Maisie. Because Maisie was there now too. She'd turned around and run back to join them. The twins had followed her.

"Bitter cookies?" said Bee. "Amy and I don't remember this story. We must have been babies. Did we eat them? Did they make us barf?"

"Tell it!" said Amy. She took Jojo's free hand and pulled her forward, out of the woods.

Bee waved at Mom. "We're coming! Don't eat all the treats!"

Behind them, Roland rustled and disappeared.

Theo let go of Jojo's hand, smiling at her as Amy tugged her forward, and Jojo's cut-up heart felt a tiny bit less sore. She looked at Theo and thought about how sometimes good friends—and sisters—listen to your stories, and they remember the things you tell them, and then when you're sad, they say them back to you. And remembering someone was a kind of magic too. It made the numberless pain of losing them hurt just a little less. "You have to come with us and meet our mom," Jojo said to Theo. "And later, I want you to tell me all about your dad—and your mom. I want to know what they're like."

Theo nodded and followed.

"Okay," said Jojo, breaking free of Amy's pulling.

"The bitter cookies. Maisie, help me remember it right, and then we can tell Mom, too. She might not know this one." Jojo took a deep breath, and as they walked the last bit of the way home, she started telling a story. "A long time ago, when the twins were babies—"

"A *very* long time ago," said Amy.

"Yes, a very long time ago . . ."

The story stretched out before them like a lawn of green grass and clover, beautiful and fragile.

Acknowledgments

Thank you, as always, to Swati Avasthi, who is the best author—and best friend—to talk through ideas with, book-related and otherwise. Thank you to Julie Dahlke, wonderful friend and the person who saved Tibbs (which is to say, Fabio) three times now. Thank you to my sisters for letting me mine our childhoods and dig out particular moments. Thank you to helpful readers: Lynne Jonelle, Gabriel Kellman, Rafael Kellman, and Joe Lee. Thank you to my agent, Tricia Lawrence, who read an early draft and told me in one word exactly what the story still needed. Thank you to Reka Simonsen for being the editor of my dreams!

Thank you to Reka's assistant, Kristie Choi, for her invaluable help with the manuscript and the flap copy; and thank you to art director Greg Stadnyk and managing editor Kaitlyn San Miguel for the care and attention they've given this book. Thank you to Erica Stahler for kind and smart copyediting. Lastly, a deep, deep thank you to Ji-Hyuk Kim for the beautiful cover: as always, your art is numinous. I only hope the book lives up to it.